Rachel Cohn &
David Levithan

Alfred A. Knopf New York

THIS IS A BORZOI BOOK PUBLISHED BY ALFRED A. KNOPF

www.randomhouse.com/teens

Library of Congress Cataloging-in-Publication Data
Cohn, Rachel.
Nick and Norah's infinite playlist / by Rachel Cohn and David Levithan. — 1st ed.
p. cm.
SUMMARY: High school student Nick O'Leary, member of a rock band, meets college-bound Norah Silverberg and asks her to be his girlfriend for five minutes in order to avoid his ex-sweetheart.
ISBN-13: 978-0-375-83531-5 (trade) —
ISBN-13: 978-0-375-93531-2 (lib. bdg.)
ISBN-10: 0-375-83531-8 (trade) — ISBN-10: 0-375-93531-2 (lib. bdg.)
[1. Rock groups—Fiction. 2. Love—Fiction. 3. New York (N.Y.)—Fiction.] I. Levithan, David. II. Title.
PZ7.C6665Ni 2006
[Fic]—dc22 2005012413

Printed in the United States of America
May 2006
10 9 8 7 6 5 4 3 2 1
First Edition

TO MARTHA AND

REAL NICK

The Acknowledgments Playlist

1. Tina Turner—"The Best" (for Jennifer Rudolph Walsh, Lisa Grubka, and Katie Glick)

2. Ray Charles—"You Are My Sunshine" (for Alicia Gordon and Bari Zibrak)

3. Lucinda Williams—"2 Kool 2 B 4-Gotten" (for Lorene Scafaria)

4. Belle & Sebastian—"Wrapped Up in Books" (for Jack Martin)

5. Prince—"Nothing Compares 2 U" (for Joe Monti)

6. Elvis Costello—"Alison" (for Allison Wortche)

7. The Cure—"Pictures of You" (for Melissa Nelson and Isabel Warren-Lynch)

8. Louis Armstrong—"A Kiss to Build a Dream On" (for all the good people of Knopf)

9. The Beatles—"Paperback Writer" (for our dear author friends)

10. Julie Andrews—"The Sound of Music" (for our loving families)

11. Rufus w/ Chaka Khan—"You Got the Love" (for Stephanie and Al)

12. Kylie Minogue—"Can't Get You Out of My Head" (for Billy and Nicolicious)

13. Jens Lekman—"You Are the Light (By Which I Travel into This and That)" (for Nick)

14. Kelly Clarkson—"Miss Independent" (for Anna)

15. Q and Not U—"Wonderful People" (for Martha)

16. The Magnetic Fields—"How Fucking Romantic" (for Nancy)

nick & norah's
INFINITE PLAYLIST

1. NICK

The day begins in the middle of the night. I am not paying attention to anything but the bass in my hand, the noise in my ears. Dev is screaming, Thom is flailing, and I am the clockwork, I am the one who takes this thing called music and lines it up with this thing called time. I am the ticking, I am the pulsing, I am underneath every part of this moment. We don't have a drummer. Dev has thrown off his shirt and Thom is careening into feedback and I am behind them, I am the generator. I am listening and I am not listening because what I'm playing isn't something I'm thinking about, it's something I'm feeling all over. All eyes are on us. Or at least that's what I can imagine in my stageblindness. It's a small room and we're a big noise and I am the nonqueer bassist in a queercore band who is filling the room with undertone as Dev sing-screams, *Fuck the Man / Fuck the Man / I really want to / Fuck the Man*. I am punctuating and I am puncturing and I am punching the air with my body as my fingers press hard into the chords. Sweat, malice, and hunger pour from me. This is release, or maybe it's just a plea for release. Dev is wailing now and Thom is crashing and even though my feet don't move I am traveling hard. I look past the light and see people shaking, people jumping around, people watching as

Dev takes the microphone into his mouth and keeps yelling the words. I throw the chords at them, I drench them in the soundwaves, I am making time so loud that they have to hear it. I am stronger than words and I am bigger than the box I'm in, and then I see her in the crowd and I fall apart.

I fucking told her not to come. While she was busy ripping me into pieces, that was the one fragment I begged to keep. *Please don't come to the shows. I don't want to see you there.* And she had said yes, and it hadn't been a lie then. But it turned into a lie at some point, because here she is, and my fingers are losing their place, and my buzz is losing its edge, and everything about me goes from crying out to just plain crying—all in the time it takes for me to see the shape of her lips. And then I see—oh fuck no—that she's not alone, that she's with some guy, and while she'll say she's come to watch me, there's no doubt in my mind that she's come so I can watch her. *It's over,* she'd said, and wasn't that the biggest lie of all? I am stumbling through the notes and Dev is onto the next verse and Thom is playing a little faster than he should, so I have to catch up as she leans into this guy and rocks her head like I'm making this music for her, when if I could, I would take it all away and give her as much silence as she's given me pain.

I try to keep up with Dev and Thom. We're called The Fuck Offs tonight, but that's a new name and it'll probably only last three gigs before Dev comes up with another. We've already been Porn Yesterday, The Black Handkerchiefs, The Vengeful Hairdressers, and None Of Your Business. I don't really use my vote, except to veto Dev's stupider ideas. ("Dude," I had to tell him, "nobody wants to see a band called *Dickache*.") Dev's out to pierce the pierced, tattoo the tattooed, and have his way with the messy punk boys who come to our shows not knowing they'll end up wanting to mess around with the guy challenging *How big is your cocker spaniel?* into the mic. Dev's from a town in Jersey called Lodi, and that makes perfect sense to me, since he's nothing if not an idol in reverse. Thom's from South Orange, and has only had an 'h' in his first name for the past two months. I'm from Hoboken, as close to the city as you can get without actually being in the city. On nights like this, with a chance to play in front of more than just our friends, I'd swim across the Hudson if I had to, in order to get to this cave of a club. At least until Tris shows up and I find myself bleeding invisibly across the stage.

Take the Power / Fuck the Man / Take the Power / and Fuck the Man. Dev is taking the song somewhere it's never been before: a fourth minute. I'm rutting now, waiting for the wind-down. Thom looks like he's on the verge of a solo, which is never a good place for Thom to be. I move my feet, turn away from her, try to pretend she's not there, which is the biggest fucking joke I've ever not laughed at. I try to get Dev's attention from the periphery, but he's too busy wiping the sweat on his chest to notice. Finally, though, he gets a burst of energy strong enough to end the thing on. So he throws out his arm and howls and I run us into the ground with a final lurch. The crowd sends us a burst of their own noise. I try to hear her voice, try to separate that single pitch from the shouts and applause. But she's as lost to me as she was the night I cried and she didn't turn back to see if I was okay. Three weeks, two days, and twenty-three hours ago. And she's already with someone else.

The next band is at the side of the stage. The owner of the club is motioning that our time is up. I am not so gone that I'm not gratified by the calls for more, by that little sound of letdown when the lights go up to show the crowd a clearer path back to the bar. I am the equipment bitch for this gig, so while Dev jumps into the crowd to find his most willing admirer and Thom blushingly retreats to his understanding-but-emo boyfriend, I have to immediately detox so I can pack up our gear. I go from chords to cords, amped to amps. One of the guys from the next band is cool and helps me recover the cases from the back corner of the stage. But I'm the only one who can touch the instruments, putting them carefully to bed for the night. Then I offer to help the new band set up, and am glad when they say yes so I can be connecting them to the soundboard instead of spending all my energy resisting her.

My eye is still used to searching for her in a crowd. My breath is still used to catching when I see her and the light is angled just right. My body is still used to hers moving next to mine. So the distance—anything short of contact—is a constant rejection. We were together for six months, and in each of those months my desire found new ways to be fueled by her. *It's over* can't kill that. All of the songs I wrote in my head were for her, and now I can't stop them from playing. This null soundtrack. *I'm tired,* she'd said, and I told her that I was tired, too, and that I wanted to take some time for us, too. And then she'd said, *No, I'm tired of you,* and I slipped into the surreal-but-true universe where we were over and I wasn't over it. She was no longer any kind of *here* that I could get to.

I keep my back to the crowd as I store the equipment and instruments somewhere safe. Then comes the moment when I can't keep my back to it anymore, since there's only so long that you can stare at a wall before you feel like an idiot. I am saved by the next band, which cranks the volume even higher and soon engulfs us all in beautiful chaos. They're called Are You Randy? and the lead singer is actually singing instead of moaning and Ramoning. I dare a glance into the crowd and I don't see her anymore. I don't see very many *her*s at all—it's a sea of hims pressing and crashing against one another as the lead singer tells them the state of things, breaking into bits and pieces of "I Want You to Want Me" and "Blue Moon" and "All Apologies" as he dances through his own seven veils.

I think Tris will like this band, and the fact that I know this stabs me again, because all the knowledge of what she likes is perfectly useless now. I wonder who the guy is. I wonder if the two of them knew each other three weeks and three days ago. I'm glad I didn't really see him because then I'd think of them naked. Now I just think of her naked, and it's such a vivid touch memory that my fingers actually move to take it in. I turn my head, as if I've been actually seeing her, and see Thom and his boyfriend Scot making out to the music in a corner-of-the-universe way. Dev, I figure, is still at the bar, still performing. We're underage, but that doesn't matter here. The crowd is mostly older than us—college or should-be-in-college—and I'm aware of not really fitting in. Some of the older guys in the crowd check me out, give me a nod. It's not like I wear a Badge of Straight or anything. I nod back sometimes, when I think it's a musical acknowledgment and not an invitation. I always keep moving.

I find Dev at the bar, talking to a guy our age who looks familiar in that Type kind of way. When I get to where they're standing, I'm introduced as "the bass god, Nick," and he's introduced as "Hunter from Hunter." Dev thanks me for being equipment bitch, and from the way the conversation doesn't continue from there I know I'm interrupting. If it was Thom, my agitation would probably be noticed. But Dev needs you to spell emotions out for him, and right now I'm not in the mood. So I just tell him where I left the stuff and pretend I'm going off to search for a clear spot on the bar to summon the bartender from. And once I'm pretending that's the truth, I figure it might as well be the truth. I still can't see Tris, and there's a small part of me that's wondering if it was even her in the crowd. Maybe it was someone who looked like Tris, which would explain the guy who didn't look like anybody.

Are You Randy? stop playing their instruments one by one, until the lead singer croons a final, a cappella note. I wish for their sake I could say the club falls into silence at this, but in truth the air is one-half conversation. Still, that's better than average, and the band gets a lunge of applause and cheers. I clap, too, and notice that the girl next to me puts two fingers in her mouth to whistle old-fashioned style. The sound is clear and spirited, and makes me think of Little League. The girl is dressed in a flannel shirt, and I can't tell whether that's because she's trying to bring back the only fashion style of the past fifty years that *hasn't* been brought back or whether it's because the shirt is as damn comfortable as it looks. She has very pale skin and a haircut that reads *private school* even though she's messed it up to try to hide it. The next band opened for Le Tigre on their last tour, and I figure this girl's here to see them. If I was a different kind of guy, I might try to strike up a friendly conversation, just to be, I dunno, friends. But I feel that if I talk to someone else right now, all I'll be able to do is unload.

Thom and Scot would probably be ready to go if I wanted them to, but I'm pretty sure Dev hasn't figured out yet whether he's coming back with us or not, and I'd be an asshole to put him on the spot and ask. So I'm stuck and I know it, and that's when I look to my right and see Tris and her new guy approaching the beer-spilled bar to order another round of whatever I'm not having. It's definitely her, and I'm definitely fucked, because the between-band rush is pressing toward me now and if I try to leave, I'll have to push my way out, and if I have to push my way out, she'll see me making an escape and she'll know for sure that I can't take it, and even if that's the goddamn truth I don't want her to have actual proof. She is looking so hot and I am feeling so cold and the guy she's with has his hand on her arm in a way that a gay friend would never, ever think of, and I guess that's my own proof. I am the old model and this is the new model and I could crash out a year's worth of time on my bass and nothing, absolutely nothing, would change.

She sees me. She can't fake surprise at seeing me here, because of course she fucking knew I'd be here. So she does a little smile thing and whispers something to the new model and I can tell just from her expression that after they get their now-being-poured drinks they are going to come over and say *hello* and *good show* and—could she be so stupid and cruel?—*how are you doing?* And I can't stand the thought of it. I see it all unfolding and I know I have to do something—anything—to stop it.

So I, this random bassist in an average queercore band, turn to this girl in flannel who I don't even know and say:

"I know this is going to sound strange, but would you mind being my girlfriend for the next five minutes?"

2. NORAH

Randy from Are You Randy? insists the bassist from the queercore band is a 'mo, but I told him No, the guy is straight. Whether or not he's responsible for his band's shit lyrics (*Fuck the Man / Fuck the Man*—what's that trite crap?), I have no idea, but he's 'no 'mo. Trust me. There are certain things a girl just knows, like that a fourth minute on a punk song is a bad, bad idea, or that no way does a Jersey-boy bassist with Astor Place hair who wears torn-up, bleach-stained black jeans and a faded black T-shirt with orange lettering that says *When I say Jesus, you say Christ,* swing down boy-boy alley; he's working the ironic punk boy–Johnny Cash angle too hard to be a 'mo. Maybe he's a little *emo,* I told Randy, but just because he doesn't look like a Whitesnake-relic-reject like all of your band, does not automatically mean the guy's gay.

The incidental fact of his straightness doesn't mean I want to be NoMo's five-minute girlfriend, like I'm some 7-Eleven quick stop on his slut train. Only because I am the one loser here who hasn't lost all her senses to beer, dope, or hormones do I have the sense to hold back my original instinct—to yell back "FUCK, NO!" in response to NoMo's question.

I have to think about Caroline. I always have to think about Caroline.

I noticed NoMo loading equipment after his band's set while his bandmates abandoned him to score some action. I understand that scene. I am that scene, cleaning up everyone else's mess.

NoMo dresses so bad—he has to be from Jersey. And if Jersey Boy is equipment bitch, he has a van. The van's probably a piece of scrap metal with a leaking carburetor that as likely as not will pop a tire or run out of gas in the middle of the Lincoln Tunnel, but it's a risk I have to take. Somebody's got to get Caroline home. She's too drunk to risk taking her on the bus. She's also so drunk she'll go home with Randy if I'm not there to take her back to my house where she can sleep it off. Groupie bitch. If I didn't love her so much, I'd kill her.

She's lucky my parents love her just as much; her dad and stepmonster are away for the weekend, they don't give a fuck what she does, so long as she doesn't get pregnant or date any boy from a non-six-figure-plus-income household. Jerk-offs. My parents, they adore Caroline, beautiful Caroline with the long caramel hair, the big cherry Tootsie Pop lips, the juvenile delinquent arrest record. They won't care if she stumbles from my room into the kitchen tomorrow afternoon all disheveled and hung over. She's the one, not me, who meets their expectation of what the daughter of an Englewood Cliffs–livin', fat-cat record company CEO should be: *wild*.

Caroline's not a Big Disappointment like their Plain Jane, comfy-flannel-shirt-wearing, tousled bowl-head-haircut-courtesy-of-a-$300-salon-visit-with-Mom-(Bergdorf's)-and-a-$5-can-of-blue-spray-paint (Ricky's), straight-edge, responsible valedictorian bitch daughter. I've chosen a gap year on a *kibbutz* in South Africa over Brown. *WHY, Norah, WHY?* I wrote my Brown admissions essay about all the music Dad appropriated from The Street then goddamned ruined to make profit for The Man. *I am not a fuckin' corporate hippie,* Dad said, laughing, after he read the essay. Dad won't deny that he's responsible for giving Top 40 radio a disproportionate percentage of its suckiest hits, yet he's proud he indoctrinated me from childhood in the sounds of every other kind of music out there so that now, at age eighteen, I can be a badass DJ when I want, but I am also an insufferable music snob. My parents have also done me the misfortune of being happily married for a quarter century, which no doubt dooms my own prospects of ever experiencing true love. Gold is not struck twice.

My parents would disown me if they knew I was in this club tonight. Hell, I could be scoring weed in Tompkins Square Park right now, on my way to a bondage bar on Avenue D, and my parents would only applaud. But this club, this is the one joint in all of Manhattan I'm supposedly forbidden from going to, owing to a long-simmering feud over a bad music deal between Dad and the club owner, Crazy Lou (who used to be my godfather, *Uncle* Lou, until all that business leading Lou to be rechristened *Crazy*). Lou's such an old punk he was around when The Ramones were junkie hustlers first and musicians second, when punk meant something other than a mass-marketing concept designed to help the bridge-and-tunnel crowd feel cool.

But Mom and Dad would move past disowning me and outright kill me if they thought I wasn't looking after their beloved Caroline. She inspires that kind of devotion in people. It's nauseating, except I am totally under Caroline's spell, too, her lead minion, have been since nursery school.

I look around the club as the between-set mass of people swarm past/through/into me like I'm a ghost with the inconvenience of malleable flesh getting in their way on the way to the beer. Damn, I've lost Caroline again. She is big on Randy tonight, which is cool—Are You Randy? don't completely suck—but Randy himself is big on E tonight, and I gotta make sure he doesn't get her alone in a corner. But I'm only 5-foot-4 on tippy toes, and 6-foot NoMo is standing in front of me, blocking my view, waiting to find out if I want to be his five-minute girlfriend and looking like that lost animal who goes around asking "Are you my mother?" in that kid book.

From behind him I don't see Caroline but I do see that stupid bitch, Tris, rhymes with *bris,* cuz that's what she'll do to a guy, rip apart his piece. She's doing her Tris strut with her big boobs sticking out in front of her, wiggling her ass in that way that gets the instant attention of every dumb schmo in her wake, even the gay boys, who seem to be highly represented here tonight, NoMo notwithstanding. She's coming right toward me. No No NOOOOOOOOOOO. How did she find out Caroline and I would be here tonight? Does she have lookouts with text pagers set up every place Caroline and I go on a Saturday night, or what?

Boyfriend to the rescue! I answer NoMo's question by

putting my hand around his neck and pulling his face down to mine. God, I would do anything to avoid Tris recognizing me and trying to talk to me.

FUCK! I didn't expect NoMo to be such a good kisser. Asshole. See this, Randy? NO. MO. Confirmed. But I am not looking for chemistry here, just a ride home for my girl. I am also not looking for tongue, but NoMo's wastes no time sliding its way into my mouth. My mouth revolts against my mind: *Umm, feels good down here, steady girl, steaaaady!*

No matter how good he tastes, this five-minute girlfriend still needs a few seconds to come up for air. I separate my mouth from his, hoping to catch my breath and hoping to catch Tris walking away from us without having noticed me after all.

WOW. I feel like in this riot of people, I have been kicked in the stomach, but by the giddy police. Forget about the need for oxygen. My mouth wants to go back to the place it just left.

Unfortunately, Tris is standing right in front of us, hanging on to her latest slobber victim, who is near enough now that I can positively ID him as one of Caroline's recent rejects; he's buddies with Hunter from Hunter, whose band, Hunter Does Hunter, is scheduled to play next (you're welcome, Hunter, for the introduction to Lou). Tris clutches her arm tight around the guy's waist, probably squeezing out whatever remaining life that soul-sucking skank hasn't yet gotten out of him in the three weeks or so since Caroline gave him the heave-ho.

Tris says, "Nick? Norah? How do you two, like, know each other?"

That bitch should not be in a club like this. As if her language is not enough indication, there is also the matter of her Hot Topic mallrat outfit: short black leather skirt with buckles up the side, mass-produced "vintage" Ramones T-shirt, and piss-yellow leggings with some horrible pair of pink patent-leather shoes. She looks like a neon sign bumblebee by way of early Debbie Harry rip-off.

I'm going to need another talk with Uncle Lou about standards *vis-à-vis* owning and operating a club. The guy can snag great new talent—the raw, hungry kind who are ready to bleed their intestines or other useful body parts onto Crazy Lou's stage for the opportunity to perform on it—but he doesn't know shit about how to run this business. Look at the underage Jersey riffraff he lets in! He probably even comps the beers for the band members! LOU! Why do you think so many of these assholes are alcoholics and junkies? They've got the music right. They can play the core punk songs with conviction—hard, fast, angry—but they haven't wised up yet to the fact that the real punk goes down now with a straight edge: no alcohol, no drugs, no cigarettes, no skanks. The real punk now is the only punk left after all the madness: the music, the message.

Well, dudes, drink up, because when I get back from South Africa next year and take over managing this club as Uncle Lou has promised instead of reapplying to Brown as I promised my parents, there's gonna be a new sheriff here on the Lower East Side, my friends. Have your lecherous, skanky fun now, because the clock is running out on you.

I may reconsider the future make-out ban, however. The

making-out part is nice, it has possibilities, with the right pair of lips.

I don't know why, but I do that thing Caroline does to her male victims, where instead of taking the hand of NoMo, I place my hand at the back of his neck and scratch the nape softly, possessively, while Tris watches. My fingers scan the buzz cut of his hair back there, and I feel goose bumps rising on his neck. I likee. There is some satisfaction in seeing Tris's bottom lip nearly fall to her chin in shock. That's the thing about Tris: She's never subtle.

Whatever I'm doing, it works. She storms away, speechless. Phew. That was easier than I expected.

I look at my watch. I believe my new boyfriend and I have about two minutes forty-five before we break up. I close my eyes and do the slight head turn, angling for another visitation from his lips.

Caroline says I am frigid. Sometimes I think she's teasing me to repeat the party line of my Evil Ex, so I clarify: *You mean I'm not easy?* She clarifies: *No, bitch, I mean you intimidate guys with a look or a comment before they can even decide if they want a chance with you. You're so judgmental. Along with frigid.*

NoMo must know this about me, because he doesn't come back in for more mouth-to-mouth contact. He says, "How the hell do you know Tris?"

Then I remember. Tris called him NICK. Nooooooooo. That's *him*! NICK! The Hoboken boy! The guy who wrote all the songs and poems about her, the best goddamn boyfriend the rest of us at Sacred Heart never had, the band-boy stud Tris hooked up with after meeting him on the PATH train at the beginning of the school year and has lied to and cheated on ever since. Does NICK not think it's weird that he dated her that long and never once met any girls from her school? IDIOT!

But of course Tris wouldn't introduce him to us. She wouldn't be worried we'd rat out her indiscretions to her boyfriend—she'd be afraid he'd fall for Caroline. Tris can have Caroline's rejects, but she'd never offer up one of her own to Caroline. Tris is so Single White Female, we like to joke that Caroline should get a restraining order against her, except Tris provides us too much amusement to completely let her out of our reach. It's like a love-hate thing we have going with her. We don't feel guilty about it because there's only a month of school left and I can't imagine we'll ever see her again after our "have a great summer, good luck in college" phony sentiment yearbook finales. And karmically, I have repaid my mean-girl debt to Tris many times over. If she passed Chemistry and Calculus this year, it's because of me. Fuck, if she graduates at all, it's because of me.

I don't bother answering Nick's question about how the hell I know Tris. I've got to find Caroline.

I stand up on the barstool. That's the only way I'll find her with all these people and this loud music and this stink sweat and this beer energy and this never-ending day that feels like it's only beginning in the middle of this night. I place my hand on Nick's head to steady my balance as I scan the crowd, and my hand can't help but rummage through his mess of hair, just a little.

There she is! I see Caroline huddling with Randy at a corner table by the brick wall just off the stage, to the right of Hunter from Hunter Does Hunter, who is now taking the mic. I don't know what song his band had prepared but the lyrics Hunter sings are clearly being made up on the spot and have nothing to do with the fast and furious guitar chords: *Dev, go home with me, Dev Dev Dev, I want you to fuck this man.*

I jump down from the barstool and take off toward Caroline, but Nick's hand clenches my wrist from behind me, pulling me back to him.

"Seriously," Nick says, "how the hell do you know Tris?"

His grip pinches the watch on my wrist, and the *ow* of the pinch turns my eyes from looking for Caroline to looking straight at him. I notice how lost he looks, yet eager for me to stay with him, his eyes kind and angry at the same time, and the noticing makes me remember a lyric from some song he wrote for Tris that she passed around in Latin class because she thought it was so lame.

The way you're singing in your sleep

The way you look before you leap

The strange illusions that you keep

You don't know

But I'm noticing

Fuck Tris. I would give body parts to have a guy write something like that for me. My kidney? Oh, both of them? Here, Nick, they're yours—just write more for me. I'll give you a start: boy in punk club asks strange girl to be his girlfriend for five minutes, girl kisses boy, boy kisses back, boy then meets girl—what did you notice about *this* girl? Nick, let's hear some lyrics. Please? Ready. Set. Go.

I want to stomp my foot in frustration—for him, and for me. Because I know that whatever Tris did or said to him, it's what's given him that haunted puppy-dog look of pathetic despair. She's the reason he will probably become an embittered old fuck before he's even of legal drinking age, distrusting women and writing rude songs about them, and basically from here into eternity thinking all chicks are lying cheating sluts because one of them broke his heart. He's the type of guy that makes girls like me frigid. I'm the girl who knows he's capable of poetry, because like I said, there are things I just know. I'm the one who could give him that old-fashioned song title of a thing called Devotion and True Love (However Complicated), if he ever gave a girl like me a second glance. I'm the less-than-five-minute girlfriend who for one too-brief kiss fantasized about ditching this joint with him, going all the way punk with him at a fucking *jazz* club in the Village or something. Maybe I would have treated him to borscht at Veselka at five in the morning, maybe I would have walked along Battery Park with him at sunrise, holding his hand, knowing I would become the one who would believe in him. I would tell him, I heard you play, I've read your poetry, not that crap your band just performed, but those love letters and songs you wrote to Tris. I know what you're capable of and it's certainly more than being a bassist in an average queercore band—you're better than that; and dude, having a drummer, it's like key, you fucking need one. I would be equipment bitch for him every night, no complaints. But no, he's the type with a complex for the Tris type: the big tits, the dumb giggle, the blowhard. Literally.

You wanted easy—well, you got it, pal.

I extract my wrist from his grip. But for some reason, instead of walking away, I pause for a moment and return my hand to his face, caressing his cheek, drawing light circles on his jaw with my index finger.

I tell him, "You poor schmuck."

3. NICK

When Tris passes by me, it's like the world is no longer three-dimensional. The third dimension falls away, then the second, and all I'm left with is one dimension, and that dimension is her.

But of course there's another dimension, too, and that dimension is time, and it keeps going and Tris keeps walking and all the other dimensions come back, and even though there are now more, it feels like a whole lot less.

And I'm left with this girl, this Siren of Mixed Signals, this Norah. She's a fuck-good kisser, but clearly has some massive consistency issues. I ask her how the fuck she knows Tris, because that is leaving me completely confused, and at first she's looking at me like I'm this guy she didn't just start kissing out of nowhere, but then she's got her hand on my arm in a way that makes me really notice I have an arm, and then she's making to run away, and at the same time looking at me like I'm some cancer child. Then I take hold of her arm and she resists without really resisting. Finally she pulls away, only to touch my face in this way that reminds me exactly of her kiss.

Then she calls me "you poor schmuck."

And like some poor schmuck, I'm like, "Why?"

I can tell she knows something, but she's not saying. Instead she tells me, "I've got to get my friend."

"I'll come with," I volunteer. I know Tris is somewhere behind me, maybe watching. And it's not like I have anything better to do than follow a fuck-good kisser wherever she wants to go. Dev is climbing onto the stage now to be Hunter's dancer, and Thom and Scot are nowhere in my line of vision.

"I'll tell you what," Norah says. "You give us a ride, and I'll give you two extra minutes on your original offer."

"Seven's my lucky number," I tell her.

And she just looks at me. *Y. p. s.*

"But really," I say. "How do you know Tris?"

"I fucked up her Barbies in fifth grade," she tells me. "And that's the way it's been ever since."

"You're from *Englewood*?"

"Englewood *Cliffs*. Englewood is the one with reasonable houses."

She's pushing through the crowd now, and I'm following.

"She was just here a second ago," she says.

"Who?"

"No one. Caroline. I mean, just shut up for a second so I can think, okay?"

Like if I'm quiet, she'll suddenly be able to hear every fucking footstep in the club.

While she's peering around, I make the idiot move of looking behind me, and see Tris and the new model making out. She looks so hot in her Ramones shirt and the gold stockings I always asked her to wear because they make her look like something out of a Marvel comic. I remember taking that shirt off of her, those stockings off of her—her yelling *careful, careful!* as I started to get past her thighs. And now it's some other guy's hands that are thumbing their way over Joey's face and down Dee Dee's chin and—oh, fucking hell—dropping down between the A and the M, going right for the V under the H&M-meets-S&M miniskirt.

And she's looking at me the whole time. I swear she's looking at me.

I turn away and Norah isn't there, but luckily she's only a few feet away. And the girl she's diving for looks kinda familiar. Not in a Didn't We Go To Camp Walla Walla Together? way, but more like, Didn't I Step Over You To Get To The Men's Room Last Night? Right now she's hanging on to the guy from Are You Randy? like she's auditioning to be a pocket on his jacket. And I can tell he's about ready to sew her on. Only my Seven-Minute Girlfriend stands in the way. She's saying Caroline's name like an older sister would say it, and from the resentment that flashes back in Caroline's eyes I'd believe they were sisters if Norah hadn't already called Caroline her friend. I also think for a millisecond that they might be a couple, but something in Norah's expression makes it clear that they're friends without benefits.

Caroline's about to say something really harsh, but suddenly Hunter and Dev launch into a fucking *Green Day* cover, and we're all seven years old again and dancing like we spit out the Ritalin while Mom wasn't looking. We become this one flailing paramecium mass, fever-connected as the guitarist riffs electrons. Even Tris must be a part of this, and if we're both a part of it, then that means we're still in some way connected. Everyone in this room is connected, except Norah—she's the kind of statue they don't ever make, a statue of someone totally defeated. Caroline's dancing against the guy from Are You Randy? like God or Billie Joe Armstrong meant her to do it. I try to obliterate myself in the song, but there's something in me that just won't combust. I think my seven-minute girlfriend is standing on the fuse.

"What's up?" I shout. And she looks at me like she's forgotten that I exist. This means she's also forgotten to guard herself from me, so I have a moment when I see the sentences behind her eyes. *I can't do this. This is too fucking hard.*

I change my question. I say, "What's wrong?" And just like that, her sentences are shut behind a screen. But I'm curious. Yes, I'm damn curious.

"Not a fucking thing," she says. "And I think maybe our time is up."

"You don't need a ride anymore?" I ask. I'm not above using my wheels to angle for some more time with a complicated girl.

"Fuck." The song's ended now and everyone is cheering. I barely hear her shout, "Wait right here."

Dev and Hunter take their bows like they're already spooning, Dev curved over Hunter's back as they dip in unison. While the guy from Are You Randy? uses his hands to clap, Norah puts her hand on Caroline's shoulder and leans in to shout in her ear. What follows is one of those ropeless tugs of war, measured in centimeters of pull and pull away. I can't hear any of it until Caroline screams, "I am not trashed!" which of course means she is, because who the hell else would use such a completely wasted phrase? The guy from Are You Randy? is starting to catch on and is trying to catch up by catching hold. But his instinct totally defeats him, because his hand swerves somewhere near her breast, which isn't really the terrain he needs to keep his ground. Norah's yank trumps his hairy palm in this contest, and Caroline is soon stumbling in my direction.

Before I really know what's happening, Caroline's tilting into me and I'm catching her. Then she's heaving down, and I'm sure she's about to puke all over me, but instead she rises and looks at me and says, "You have really ugly shoes."

Norah's next to me now, saying, "Let's go." She leaves Caroline there for me to carry as she yells, "Get the fuck out of my way" to people, uncrowding them with her snarl. My heart understands the direction we're going in, because it starts pounding like it's got something really damn important to say, and by the time I'm out of my head enough to really use my eyes, there's someone in our way, and that someone is the girl who took the key to my heart and swallowed it with a smile.

"I need your car," she says.

And it's like I've forgotten that the word for "What?" is "What?" because I just stand there and look at Tris and think *she's talking to me* and somehow translate that into *she's giving me a chance.*

"I need to go somewhere," she tells me. "I promise I'll bring it back."

I'm reaching for the keys in my pocket. I'm thinking *I'll go with you*. I'm thinking of passenger-seat conversations and making song dedications in my head. Her face lit by that nighttime driving light—two parts dashboard, one part headlight strobe from the opposite lane. I am remembering that so much.

Fuck, I loved her then. And *then* is blurring into *now*. I'm thinking *why not?* I'm thinking *we're still the same people*. And a voice outside of me is saying, "I'm afraid the car's already full. No room for you, *Tris*. Sorry."

This Norah girl's grinning now, all transparent sweetness and light.

"Excuse me?" Tris asks.

"I'm sorry. I wasn't clear. Let me try again. FUCK OFF."

"I think turning off to fucking is *your* department, Norah. Now why don't you take Drunkzilla here and go find some nice Weezer fans to rock-tease. I'm talking to Nick, not you."

And I'm thinking: *She's fighting over me. Tris is fighting over me.*

But for some reason it's Norah who's putting her arm around me and putting her hand in my back pocket.

I'm about to shudder her off, but then Tris says, "Come on, Nick—we're really late and need the car. I'll pay you back for the gas." And I know right away that I'm not a part of her "we." I've been fucking exiled from her "we."

"I'm going to find Randy," Caroline decides.

"Hell, no, you're not," Norah says, taking her arm from my shoulder and linking it around Caroline's elbow. Which leaves us in this weird *we're off to see the Wizard* pose, with Tris blocking us like the Wicked Witch of the Past.

She could have me so easily. But instead she snorts and says, "You can take him. I only wanted his car."

And with that, Tris leaves me for good. Every time I see her, from now until I die, she will leave me for good. Over and over and over again.

Norah takes her hand out of my back pocket and steadies Caroline with her full body. It's my turn to lead now, and I can barely do it. It's not that I'm drunk or stoned or spiraling high. It's just that I'm defeated. And that's impairing all of my senses.

There's only one hopeful chord in this cacophony, and it's this girl I'm following. I know I could tell her to get a cab—I have a feeling she can more than afford it—but I like the idea of leaving with her and staying with her. She says good-bye to the club manager as we reach the door and are released onto the street. The sidewalk is full of smokers, talking or posing their way to ash. I get the nod from a couple of people I vaguely know. Ordinarily if I left with two hot girls, there'd also be some looks of admiration. Maybe it's because of the clear anger between Norah and Caroline, or maybe it's because they all think I'm gay—whatever the case, I get no more congratulations than a cabdriver does for picking up a fare.

I know I should offer to help Norah propel Caroline forward, but the truth is that I don't feel like I can carry anyone but myself right now. The streets are empty. I am empty. Or, no—I am full of pain. It's my life that's empty.

I stumble for my keys. Tris will not be waiting for me inside the car. Tris will not be waiting for me ever again.

I shouldn't have come here. I shouldn't have been anywhere that she could find.

We're at my car.

"What the fuck is *that*?" Norah asks.

I shrug and say, "It's a Yugo."

4. NORAH

So this is what my promising life has been reduced to. The Jewish princess from Englewood Cliffs, fucking valedictorian who *chose* a Catholic girls' high school to accompany her best friend through the experience, who *chose* to turn down Brown, the girl whose possibilities now that she's about to be let loose upon the world should supposedly be infinite, is sitting through the middle of an April night in the passenger side of a Yugo that smells like Tris's patchouli aromatherapy oil. Perhaps it's only the vehicle that won't start, but it feels like it's my life that won't start. Yes, this Yugo with the passenger-side seat metal coming through the torn seat fabric, scratching against the back of my thigh, this Cold War relic that won't respond to Nick's turn of the ignition key, is like a fucking metaphor for my sorry-ass life: STALLED.

Nick might be a bass god but he's also a parking god because he scored a spot right in front of the club, the unfortunate consequence of which is that now my stalled ears are receiving the listening benefit of the band playing inside the club and they're really fucking good and that's really pissing me off. I'm not sure if I backed into my life by getting into this Yugo with my new almost-boyfriend, or if I backed out of it by leaving the club to save Caroline once again, but whichever end it is, I'm left wanting more music. It's still Hunter on the stage but now I can hear that the Dev dude is singing some strange harmony with Hunter on another Green Day cover, "Time of Your Life." Hunter Does Hunter have accelerated the lite-FM classic song (because how much more punk can you go than producing an elevator song staple—bless you, Billie Joe) up to Parliament tempo and I swear there's a DJ mixing a sample of that Michael Jackson freak moaning about how *Billie Jean is not my lover, the kid is not my son* into the groove. How is that possible and why does it sound so damn good and if the Yugo doesn't start within one second I am outta here, I don't care how tempted I am to try for another seven minutes of being Nick's girlfriend after we've got Caroline back to my place. For a poor schmuck, he's temptatiously fucking cute.

"Do you hear that?" I ask Nick.

"What? Is the engine starting?" The poor schmuck is not only cute and a great head-bob thrash-dancer, he's probably a good guy. At least he proved deft at maneuvering a drunken Caroline goddess into the backseat of a freakin' Yugo and making her think it was her idea. Let's not forget the part about him being a great kisser. He deserves better than a Tris—and a Yugo.

I tell him, "No. Dude. Listen up, that rhythmic banging inside the club? It's called drumming. It's, like, famous as an underlying staple of sound since primitive cultures." I play drums on the glove compartment of the Yugo. The compartment pops open from my banging. A Polaroid of Tris is taped inside the compartment. I rip it out. Bloody hell! Caroline isn't paranoid—Tris really *did* swipe Caroline's vintage cut-off white T-shirt with Flea's autograph over the left breast area. I toss the picture out the window and turn to face Nick. "Your fucking band needs a drummer. I saw you grinding to Hunter's earlier Green Day cover of 'Chump' back in the club. I know you feel rhythm more than just your heart-attack-inducing bass skills. Think about it. What would 'Chump' have been without Tres Cool? Get a drummer for your band, guy. Really."

Caroline has yet to reach her warm-cuddly drunk stage, post-heave and pre-slumber, which would put her in inquisitive stage about now, and right on schedule, from the backseat, she interjects, "Really," because Caroline is always picking up sentences where I leave 'em off. "Driver person. Hey!" She taps Nick's shoulder from behind him. Nick looks around to her but quickly turns back around to face me. Such a pretty girl, such rancid tequila breath. Caroline wants to know, "Why would you wear such ugly shoes? Answer me, driver person. Please?"

"The shoes go with the car, Caroline," I tell her. "Yugo drivers are required to wear torn-and-graffitied hi-top Chucks shit on their feet. It's like a rule. It's in the manual." I pull the Yugo car manual from the glove compartment. A chewed-up wad of gum extends from the manual back to the compartment. I take the McDonald's napkin stuck inside the compartment and wipe the gum away from the manual. Fucking Tris and her Bubblicious. I throw the manual into the backseat for Caroline's perusal.

She ignores the Good Book. "Are you Yugoslavian, driver person?" Caroline asks Nick. "Norah, is that why's he's driving us home? He's the taxi driver, right?"

"Sure," I tell her. He'll be the taxi driver as soon as his Yugo-cab will fucking start. We're operating on a limited window of opportunity here. It took ten minutes just to get Caroline into the backseat. I can see Randy now, loitering outside the club, smoking a cigarette, talking up Crazy Lou but glancing toward the Yugo, ready to pounce on Caroline again, I'm sure, if this Yugo doesn't blow outta here soon.

"Is there such an ethnicity as Yugoslavian anymore?" Nick asks. "Now that the country's all broken up? That was some bad shit that went down there in Serbia and Croatia, right? Damn shame." He shakes his head and his hand idles on the ignition key, as if he's given up. He knocks his head against the wheel, then slams his fist against the stick shift. He's done. Can't take it anymore. This car ain't going nowhere. He looks so depressed and defeated, I don't have the heart to slam him for acting like he's grieving for Yugoslavia when it's so obvious he's really grieving for Tris.

Caroline informs us, "I'm part Yugoslavian, you know. On my great-grandpa's side."

I tell her, "You're part Transylvanian, too, bitch. Be quiet. I need to think." How the hell are we going to get home now? And why do I have to get Caroline home, anyway? There's a hot guy sitting next to me, even if he is a Tris pass-along, but he's got potential to be molded. Here I am in Manhattan, like Dad's favorite Stevie Wonder song goes: *New York, just like I pictured it—skyscrapers, and everythang.* Shit is supposed to be *happening* here, not stalled Yugo shit. Through the car windshield, I can see the Empire State Building, lit up in pink and green for Easter. I am reminded that Jesus died for Caroline's sins, not mine—I'm from a different tribe—so why am I saving her ass again when I could be outside this Yugo getting some life-living going on? I never properly used up those two add-on minutes of being Nick's girlfriend.

Caroline says, "You're not the boss of me, Sub Z."

It's basic instinct, I can't help myself. I turn around to face Dragonbreath and snap, "Don't call me that!" She giggles, satisfied to have gotten a rise out of me.

Caroline's giggling mercifully transforms to dozing. In the reflection off the passenger-side mirror, I see that Caroline appears to be falling asleep, her cheek pressed against the backseat window. I've never seen her pass out without heaving first. Nick and his Yugo may have magical properties, after all. Please, let it last till we can make it back to Jersey.

A heave-snore from the backseat announces that Caroline is indeed out. YES! Sweet Jesus, thank you—for this temporary stay, and hey, I'll throw in thanks for the dying-for-my-sins thing, too. You ROCK, J.C.! I'm totally gonna not stress on the fact that once I get home, I'll have to sleep next to Dragonbreath to make sure she doesn't choke on her own vomit in her sleep. Again.

"That's one problem solved," I tell Nick. I place my left hand on his right hand, which is clutched around the stick shift. "Now, what are we gonna do about this other one?"

He flinches a little at my touch and pulls his hand away to

turn the ignition key again. Don't know why I placed my hand on his anyway.

He wants to know, "Why would you fuck up Tris's Barbies?" and now I'm like, Shit, is this the price of the sacrifice for Caroline passing out unexpectedly early—that Nick has taken over the melancholy stage that usually follows Caroline's inquisitive one? "I have three sisters and I know that's some serious business, messing with another girl's Barbies." Okay, maybe he's not being melancholy because his sarcastic smile lets me know he's back to being standard-issue bandboy irony creature. Damn him that it somewhat makes me wanna jump his bones.

Still, I can tell he's looking for information, but I am not going into the Tris thing with him. I just can't. Sub Z can only do so much damage to the male psyche in one night.

On the other hand, perhaps I could make a project out of Nick, detox him from Tris, rehabilitate him, put him through a good-girlfriend immersion program. I like sevens—we could go steady like all sweet and nice, for seven days instead of minutes. Then I'll set him free, less the Tris baggage, molded and perfected into the great guy I know he is under those Tris-heavy eyes. He'll be my gift to womankind, an ideal male specimen of musicianship and making out. I'll send him back out into the world thoroughly cleansed of irony, no longer holding all females in contempt as potential Tris suspects. Now who rocks, J.C.?

A white van barrels down the one-way street in the wrong direction, stopping in front of the fire hydrant directly ahead of the Yugo.

"Oh, thank God," Nick says. Interesting. We're in tune on the divine intervention thing. Fate?

A guy emerges from the van and I recognize him as the guy who made out with the non-singing member of Nick's band after their band's set. I only caught a minute of their kissing before I had to look away. Sub Z is way turned on by two boys kissing. I don't see why ogling same-sex kissing should be the exclusive domain of frat boys whacking off to lesbian action, that's so sexist. Feminism should be all-inclusive—it should be about sexual liberation, equal pay for equal work, and the fundamental girl right of boy2boy appreciation.

If not for the really hot kissing I witnessed between those two guys, I might not have answered Nick's request to be his five-minute girlfriend by pulling his mouth down to mine. That seems like years ago, not minutes, what with Dragonbreath and the stalled Yugo since, and WHY am I giving so much thought to being suspended in time and in Yugo with this Nick guy, anyway? He's hung up on TRIS!

The boyfriend of the band guy—he's so emo he's practically a Muppet—leans into Nick's open window. He tells Nick, "Pop the hood and we'll try to jump-start this baby."

"Yeah," Nick says, like it's their routine. "Thanks, Scot."

Scot looks my way. He says, "Thom could use some help in the van if you don't mind."

What the fuck? Whatever.

I shrug and get out of the Yugo while Scot pops the Yugo hood to attach the jumper cables. I pass Randy leaning against the wall of the club and I give him a shove, just because. Then I step to the passenger side of the van and see band equipment in the back. I *knew* Nick's band had a van! Why didn't I specify—*van,* not Yugo, back to Jersey?

The guy sitting in the driver side of the van says, "Hi. I'm Thom. With an 'h.' "

I tell him, "I'm Gnorah. With a 'g.' The 'g' is silent. Like 'gnome.' "

"Really?" T**h**om says.

"No, not really. I have an 'h' too. At the end. Used to be just N-O-R-A but then I had the H legally added to my name after my dad failed to sign up Norah Jones when he had the chance. I don't like him to forget these things easily."

"Really?" T**h**om says again.

Not really. "Really," I say. "But I can't imagine why I am in this van to talk about H's. What's up?"

T**h**om hands me a crumpled fifty-dollar bill. He says, "Scot and I chipped in. We saw that kiss between you and Nick." T**h**om's not the singer of their band, but he nevertheless can channel the Aretha, not En Vogue, version of a song when he sings out, *"Giving him something he can feel!"*

"I don't get it," I say.

The hood of the van obstructs our view, but we can hear the rattle of the Yugo engine threatening to come to life. "No time to explain," T**h**om says. "Let's just say Scot and I hate the fucking guts of Nick's ex and we'd like to give him a little assistance with moving on with his life. So, please, take the boy out tonight, see the city, see the backseat of the Yugo, I don't care, just please take our friend out tonight. We've already decided that we like you and that you'll be Nick's salvation. No pressure or anything."

Flattery could get him everywhere and I am all about salvation right now, but, "Can't," I tell him, though I'm tempted. Really tempted. I'm curious what would happen if I dared another leap toward Nick's hand—or other parts, like that really tasty NoMo mouth. "Nick's giving me and my drunk friend a ride back to Jersey. She's asleep in the back of the Yugo now."

T**h**om says, "We've got a mattress in the back of the van. We'll trade you. We'll get her home if you'll take on Nick tonight."

I decide some living is worth doing. "Done," I tell him. I slip the fifty into my inside shirt pocket, then scribble the directions to my house on T**h**om's hand. I tell him where to find the house key under the potted plant and not to worry about my parents—they'll probably tip him for getting Caroline home and making me go out on a date with a live male. And I am not feeling frigid about Nick at all. I can't remember the last time I felt anticipation—not of sex (necessarily), but of getting to know a delicious new person, even if he is a poor schmuck.

So we're settled, and I get out of the van with T**h**om, who enlists Scot to help him transport Caroline from the Yugo to the van. But once I'm back inside the Yugo, I have no chance to explain to Nick the new order of this middle of the night.

Because through the windshield, I see that Randy at the

wall is doing the soul-brother shake with a new arrival who happens to be the mind-fucking guy who turned me Sub Z last year. Apparently Uncle Lou's actual nephew did not survive his year on the *kibbutz* in South Africa. The call of the real wild—Manhattan—must have been too great for him. And fuck, the Evil Ex has seen me and now he's at my side at the passenger door of the Yugo and he's saying, "Hey, baby, you ready to pick up where we left off?"

5. NICK

I never thought Jessie would betray me like this. I have done nothing but love her and treat her right. I've stood by her side and defended her when people called her trash and said they didn't understand why I kept her. I thought that meant something. But no. Now when I need her most, she's totally bailed. I turn the key and I turn the key and I turn the key and she doesn't do a damn thing. How alone am I right now? Even my car has decided to give up on me.

I could be really mad at her. But mostly I'm afraid. That this is it—terminal. That we can volt her till the lights go out in Manhattan, and she'll just sit here. Unblinking. I can't afford to fix her again. If this is it, then this is *really* it.

I'm not really paying attention when Scot and Thom remove Caroline from my backseat. After all the time it took to get her in. But I can understand the impulse to abandon ship.

I'm about to help Scot connect the cables when this guy I've never seen before leans into Norah's window and says, "Hey, baby, you ready to pick up where we left off?"

What. the. fuck?

Okay, maybe I hang with a queercore crowd and all, but still—I never, ever, in a million zillion years would have imagined that a guy could use the phrase "hey, baby" and mean it.

He says it like he's whistling at some girl's boobs as she walks down the street. Who does that?

I expect Norah to put him right in his place. But instead she freezes. She *looks away,* as if she can ignore her way out of it. By some logic, this should mean that she's now looking at me, since I'm 180 degrees away from our uninvited guest. But instead she focuses on the dashboard, on the place where the lighter should be. And I guess I'm a little surprised, because it was just starting to look like we were going to go someplace together. That this wasn't just going to be a ride home. Now it's becoming a ride nowhere, and I'm sad that it's so out of my hands.

"Baby, I'm back," the guy goes on. "How 'bout getting out of this heap and saying hello?"

Now, it's one thing to try to harass Norah out of my passenger seat. But to bring Jessie into it is completely uncalled for.

"Can I help you?" I ask.

He keeps looking at Norah as he talks to me. "Yeah, buddy. I just got back to the States and I've been looking for this lady here. Can you spare her for a second?"

He reaches in the window, unlocks the door, and opens it.

"We'll be right back," he goes on. And I'm about to tell Norah she doesn't have to do a thing. But right then she reaches over and pops off her seatbelt. I figure this is a decision on her part . . . until she fails to follow it up with another movement. She just stays in the car.

"Baby . . . ," he purrs as he reaches in for her, as if she's a kid in a car seat. "I've missed you so much."

I turn the key in the ignition. Still no start. Scot comes over to my window, looks inside the car, and says, "Problem here?"

Now it's *Scot* that Norah looks at. And for some reason, this snaps her back.

"Tal," she says with an edge usually reserved for cutlery, "you haven't missed me for one fucking minute. You have never for one single second in your entire pathetic life missed me. You might have missed fucking with my head, and you might have missed the satisfaction you so clearly got from demolishing me, but those are your emotions you're missing, not mine. I'm afraid I can't help you."

"C'mon, baby," Tal says, leaning into her. She flinches back into the seat. I can sense Scot about to say something, but I beat him to it.

"Dude, nobody puts *baby* in a corner," I say. "Get the fuck out of my car."

Tal holds his hands up, steps out of the doorway.

"Just giving the lady a choice," he says. "I didn't realize she was already ruining another guy's life. I hope you have better luck than I did."

"Asshole," Norah murmurs.

Tal laughs. "Piece of shit car: five dollars. Value of Norah's opinion: three cents. Irony of her calling me an asshole: *priceless*."

"Go. Away," Norah says.

"What? Are you afraid I'm going to tell the truth?" Tal looks at me now. "Don't be fooled, partner. She talks a great game, but when you actually get to the field, you realize it's fucking *empty.*"

From somewhere beyond the hood, Thom yells, "Gentleman, start your engine!"

I cannot find a way to pray to God or some higher being. But I damn well feel comfortable praying to Jessie, and right at this moment I give her my evangelical all.

Please start. I will buy premium gas for the next month if you please, please, please start.

I turn the key in the ignition. There's a slight catch. And then . . .

Jessie's talking to me again. And she's saying, *Let's get the hell out of here.*

"I'd love to stay and chat," I say to Tal, "but we've got somewhere to be."

"Fine," Tal says, shutting the door more gently than I would've expected. "Just don't say I never warned you. You're dating the Tin Woman here. Look for a heart, you'll only come up with dead air."

"Thanks for the tip!" I say with mock cheer.

He reaches in the window and touches Norah on the cheek, holding there for a moment.

"Baby, it's you," he says. Then he turns back to the sidewalk and heads right into the club.

"Seems like a nice guy," I say. Norah doesn't respond.

Scot leans in my window now.

"Don't worry about her friend," he says. "We'll get her home. You two kids have fun now, you hear?"

"Sure thing," I tell him, even though Norah looks like the only use she has for the word *fun* is to make the word *funeral*.

Thom shuts the hood and gives me a thumbs-up. Then he and Scot walk hand in hand back to the van, the jumper cables dangling over their shoulders like a boa.

Norah hasn't moved to put her seatbelt back on. I don't know what this means. She turns to look at the door to the club.

"You okay?" I ask.

"I honestly have no idea," she says.

I put Jessie into reverse and give our parking space away to whoever comes next. It gives me some satisfaction to know that my departure will become somebody else's good luck.

It's only when I've pulled out onto the street that I realize I have no idea where we're going.

"Do you want me to take you home?" I ask.

I take her silence as a no. Because wanting to go home is the kind of thing you speak up about.

I follow up with, "What do you want to do?"

This seems to me to be a pretty straightforward question. But she looks at me with this total incomprehension, like she's watching footage of the world being blown up, and I'm the little blurb on the corner of the screen saying what the weather is like outside.

I try again.

"You hungry?"

She just holds her hand to her mouth and looks out the front windshield.

"You thirsty?"

For all I know, she's counting the streetlamps.

"Know any other bands playing?"

Tumbleweed blowing down the armrest between us.

"Wanna watch some nuns make out?"

Am I even speaking out loud?

"Maybe see if E.T. is up for a threeway?"

This time she looks at me. And if she isn't exactly smiling, at least I think I see the potential for a smile there.

"No," she says. "I'd much rather watch some nuns make out."

"Okay, then," I say, swerving the car back toward the Lower East Side. "It's time for a little burlesque."

I say this with some authority, even though I have only the faintest of faint ideas of where I'm going. Dev once told me about this place where strippers dressed like nuns and did this tease to "Climb Ev'ry Mountain." And that was only one of the acts. I figured it was too kitsch to be pervy—and that seemed to be Norah's range right there. As far as I could tell.

As we're driving across Houston, Norah reaches over and turns on the radio. A black-lipsticked oldie: The Cure, "Pictures of You"—track four of my Breakup Desolation Mix.

This, and every other song on this disc, is dedicated to Tris. . . .

And if this is the soundtrack, my mind and my broken heart collaborate to provide me with the movie—that night she was so tired she said she needed to lie down, so she climbed over the seat and laid out in the back. I thought I'd lost her, but then five minutes later my cell phone rang and it was her, calling me from my own backseat. In a sleepy voice she told me how safe and comfortable she felt, how she was remembering all those late-night drives back from vacation, and how she'd stretch herself out and feel like her parents were driving her bed, nothing unusual about the movement of the road under the wheels and the tree branches waving across the windshield. She said those moments made her feel like the car was home, and maybe that's how I made her feel, too.

Eventually she fell asleep, but I kept the phone against my ear, lulled by her breathing, and her breathing again in the background. And yes, it felt like home. Like everything belonged exactly where it was.

"I so don't need this right now," Norah says. But she doesn't change the song.

"Have you ever thought about their name?" I ask, just to make conversation. "I mean, for what?"

"What are you talking about?"

"The Cure. What do they think they're the cure for? Happiness?"

"This coming from the bassist for *The Fuck Offs*?"

And I can't help it. I think, *Wow, she knows our name.*

"Dev's thinking of changing it to The Fuck Ons," I tell her.

"How 'bout simply Fuck On?"

"Maybe one word? Fuckon?"

"The Friendly Fuckons?"

"My Fuckon Or Yours?"

"Why is he such a fucking Fuckon?"

I look at her. "Is that a band name or a statement?"

"He had no right to do that. None."

We break into silence again. I lob a question right into it.

"Who is he, then?"

"An ex," she says, slumping back in the seat a little. "*The* ex, I guess."

"Like Tris," I say, relating.

She sits up and gives me a purely evil glance. "No. Not like Tris at all. This was real."

I pause for a second, listen to our breakup playing under the conversation.

"That was mean," I say. "You have no idea."

"Neither do you. So let's drop it. I'm supposed to show you a good time."

I take this last sentence as a kind of apology. Mostly because that's what I want it to be.

I'm winding through the Lower East Side now, on the streets that have names and not numbers. The night is still very much young here, hipster congregants exhaling their smoke from sidewalk square to sidewalk square. I find a parking space on the darker side of Ludlow, then convince Norah to retrace Jessie's steps until we're in front of a pink door.

"Camera Obscura?" Norah asks.

I nod.

"Bring on the nuns," she says.

I'm not sure if I'm supposed to knock or just open the door. The answer is given to me in the form of a burly bouncer dressed in a Playboy Bunny outfit.

"ID?" he asks.

I reach for my cousin's license from Illinois, won in a particularly intense Xbox challenge.

Norah pats her pockets down. Blankly.

And just as I think, *Oh fuck,* she says those exact words.

6. NORAH

Oh fuck. FUCK FUCK FUCK FUUUUUUUUUCK!!!!!!!

I mailed the letter turning down the acceptance to Brown just this morning. And only now, in the middle of this night or is it morning and why does time cease to tick when I see Tal, only now do I get it. *Kibbutz* in South Africa: BIG FUCKING MISTAKE. Like, HUGE. What was I thinking? So we've broken up five times over the last three years. Somehow in the back of my mind was the thought that either (1) Tal and I would work things out next time, and what better place to do that than away from our families and friends in a commune on the flip side of the world, or (2) we wouldn't work things out yet again, but I'd be the best freakin' worker that *kibbutz* had ever seen; and as a bonus, Tal would die of jealousy when I fell madly in love with some beautiful surfer boy from Capetown and left Tal weeding gardens while I bailed on the *kibbutz* to backpack across the world with my new surfer love who hopefully would have a pretty-looking name like Ndgijo.

Except that would never happen to me. How did such a reputedly smart girl get herself in this predicament, on the brink of adulthood, with no future to grab on to? These last few weeks I've been missing Tal as much as I've been bemoaning him as the Evil Ex. I've held on to the hope of surprising him by showing up in South Africa, yet when he was RIGHT THERE in front of me in Manhattan, what did I do? I froze. Suddenly all my fantasies of reconciliation were gone, suddenly all I could remember was how I was never good enough for him, Jewish enough, political enough, committed enough. Tal wasn't a lying cheating skank like Tris, but who had I been kidding? He had been, as Caroline likes to remind me, a "controlling fuckface." So right there, in a fucking Yugo, next to the poor schmuck I introduced myself to by making out with him, I finally had the moment of clarity that Mom and Dad and Caroline have been waiting for me to have since I was fifteen: ENOUGH! Caroline has been right all along. Tal and I are better off living our lives apart from one another.

Oh fuck. Did I just say that aloud? I'm trying to pay attention to the Nick guy but I can't get Tal's words in front of the club off repeat playback in my mind: *She talks a great game, but when you actually get to the field, you realize it's fucking empty.*

The Tin Woman! Tal called me the fucking Tin Woman! I lost my virginity and my whole youth to him, and that's his review of me? At least I can be grateful that when Tal took off from South Africa back to Manhattan without telling anybody, he couldn't possibly have received my letter yet; I only just mailed it. I was so hell-bent on the sentiment, I posted the letter international fucking snail mail when I could have just e-mailed him. I drew smiley faces on the outside of the envelope! Oh, God, I want to be sick right now.

Norah, why are you such a regression bitch? One night last weekend spent holding Caroline's hair back while she puked in the toilet, feeling lonely and lost—for me, not for Caroline; she had an army of dudes outside the bathroom waiting for her to sober up—and I let the dark side of my mind, the Tal side, win out. As Caroline slept it off later that night in the extra twin bed that's been in my room for her since kindergarten, I wrote to Tal. Was it all the caffeine I consumed riding the night out with Caroline, or the leftover ganja haze of the reggae club where we'd passed the night? Secondhand smoke may be deadlier than firsthand straight-edge inhale, at least when it comes to impairing my ability to distinguish between lonely longing for the Evil Ex and actually trying to get back together with him.

I hope Tal never finds out the Tin Woman was ready to compromise. I didn't outright say I wanted to get back together. But I said I was willing to consider it. I told him I could be vegan. I could be more Jewish. I could be kosher fucking vegan! I could learn to care about saving the sea otter and only drinking fair-trade coffee. I could believe that Tal and his brothers in Tel Aviv actually have talent and will become the next big thing, an older, punk-infused, pro-Israel, fuck-Europe, politicized version of Hanson. I would at least consider living with his miserable controlling psychotic mother in Tel Aviv once Tal starts his mandatory Israeli Army service next year, and oh alright fine, she could teach me how to cook the meals he likes and how to hang linens on a line in the sun so his sheets would always be crisp and fresh.

That fucking letter! Shit! I was like Saddam Hussein in the *South Park* movie, professing to Satan, *I can change! I can change!*

No. I can't change. I shouldn't change.

Caroline may be a lush and a slut but she's not a complete moron. She begged me not to post the letter, but I wouldn't listen to her. "What the fuck do you have to change for?" she said. "*He* should fucking change, uptight bastard. Why are you doing this? If you need some end-of-adolescence protest, couldn't you like just wreck your dad's Jaguar on the Palisades Parkway or something? Are you really going to put us through you and Tal, the nightmare couple, one more time? And lose out on Brown for it? Norah, you know you'll meet someone else, don't you?" Only I didn't believe her—until tonight.

What good is Caroline now, passed out in Nick's friend's van? I wonder if her cell is turned on. I need to tell her Tal is back! And I fucked up but now I have officially woken the fuck up.

"Norah?" the Playboy Bunny bouncer responds to my pronouncement of *oh fuck,* which is no small relief because I don't have a fake ID. When your dad is the well-known head of a major record label, it tends not to be necessary at most clubs in Lower Manhattan.

"Toni?" I say. S/he grabs me in a hug. Toni interned for Dad last year while deciding whether s/he wanted to pursue a career in the music industry; s/he was also my biggest advocate in my futile campaign (thus far) to convince Dad to produce an all-punk band tribute album to the Spice Girls. "Still working on that demo?"

S/he pulls out a CD strapped inside the bushy tail at her back. "Just finished it! Will you pass it on?"

"Sure," I say, hoping Nick will not interrogate me about who am I, some eighteen-year-old flannel-shirt-wearing B&T girl, to be passing on demos.

"Go right on over to the VIP area," Toni says. "I'll make sure your drinks are on the house."

"I don't drink," I remind Toni.

"Oh, live a little," s/he says, bumping me at the hip. "Miss Straight Edge, bend 'round the corner for once in your life." Toni turns to Nick. "Illinois? Twenty-three years old? Give me a fucking break. But have fun, kids."

S/he gives Nick a playful slap on the ass as we walk in and Nick doesn't react like Tal, who would have pounced back at a drag queen daring to touch him. Instead, Nick laughs and turns back around to return the gesture on Toni's ass. S/he gives him a butt shimmy dance in return. "I like this one, Norah!" s/he says. "Big improvement. Good egg."

As opposed to what—nasty, fermented egg, the kind one naturally would assume Tris would pass off?

We sit down at a small table that miraculously vacated of bodies as we approached it. For fuck's sake, my heart actually flutters for a moment when Nick pulls out the wooden chair for me. Who does that? And why does that simple gesture for a moment make me forget I am REALLY PISSED OFF and MY LIFE IS OVER. I am distracted from my Tal malaise by the nuns making out to "Climb Ev'ry Mountain" on the stage, and find myself chuckling, all of a sudden having a mental image of me and Nick in a threeway with E.T. I feel the crack of a smile on my lips and a non-frigid buzz spreading through my body. In the flashing neon lights, and with the distraction of the stage show, I finally have the opportunity to truly appraise Nick. I admire his vintage gas station attendant jacket with the name "Salvatore" stenciled under the Texaco logo, and I admit to wanting to run my fingers through his mod mess of shag hair. He seems to have an ironic but sweet half-smile stenciled on his face, despite his Tris hangover.

Nick waves thanks in Toni's direction at the door. He says, "Nice seats your friend hooked us up with. I have to admit, between your drunk girlfriend and your Yugo-insulting ex-boyfriend, it's a relief to see you have some nice friends." He winks at me and why won't that kind smile leave his face because I know if we are ever going to make it through this night/morning/whatever we have going, eventually I am going to have to tell him about Tris and that smile will be gone and I don't want to be the person responsible for killing it.

I don't owe him an explanation or anything but I do say, "I'm sorry about Tal." Only what I'm really sorry about is what I said about Tris, but I can't find it in myself to speak that apology. Yet.

Nick tells the cocktail bunny who approaches our table to please bring us drinks with little umbrellas in them, we don't care what, we're from Jersey, we won't know the difference anyway. He says to please just make sure the drinks are of the virgin variety.

Then he turns to me and says, "I don't drink. I'm pretty straight edge. I hope that's not a problem for you."

I'm only "pretty" straight edge myself. I mean, I don't drink or smoke or do drugs, but I'm not over the top about it like some of the straight-edge breed who also don't eat meat or have sex, either. My straight-edginess is rather like my Judaism: firm, but reform.

I mean to answer Nick with, "It's not a problem for me. It's a fucking miracle." But I think I end up just doing some inane yes/no head-bob of shock.

Whoa! Tris dated a straight-edge boy, and one who says *please*? How did he survive her without being drunk or stoned, like the rest of them? I'm not sure whether to admire or pity Nick for being a fellow straight edge, but I am stoked, too. I'm on a date with a guy who can have a good time without trying to get wasted? The universe is full of surprises. Respect to Tris.

"Want to tell me about it?" Nick asks once the bunny has hopped away.

"About what?"

"The Ex?"

Is this what happens on dates? You kiss before you've met, then talk about why your previous relationship failed? I'm stumped. The only guy I've ever been with is Tal, and his idea of a date was watching *Schindler's List* in his dorm room at Columbia. Besides the random incident with Nick,

I've never even truly kissed anyone besides Tal, unless you count Becca Weiner at summer camp when I was thirteen, which I don't. I have no idea how to do this "date" thing. This must be the reason I am frigid.

I really don't want to talk about Tal. I want to forget I ever entertained the notion of getting back together with him. I want to forget I've thrown away my future and that now I have to come up with a whole new plan. So I tell Nick, "I know how to drive a stick shift." Because I know Tris can't.

"So you're saying you could drive Jessie back to Jersey tonight, assuming she'll start again?"

"Who's Jessie?"

"My Yugo."

"You have a name for your Yugo? Please don't tell me you're one of those guys who also names his dick."

"Unfortunately, I've yet to find the perfect name for mine, so it's in this netherworld of nameless identity right now." Nick glances down at his crotch, then back at me. "But if you think up a good name, let me know. We'd like something a little exotic, like maybe Julio."

Frigid can thaw, right?

Nick adds, "Dev wanted to name our band Dickache. What do you think?"

"Sorry, I'm stuck on The Fuck Offs. Catchy. The sales reps at Wal-Mart will love it."

Our conversation is interrupted by a new act on the stage. Two of Toni's soul sisters are doing an onstage grind to "Edelweiss," making the previous nun performers seem like . . .

well, nuns. Nick stands up and offers his hand to me. I have no idea what he wants, but what the hell, I take his hand anyway, and he pulls me up on my feet then presses against me for a slow dance and it's like we're in a dream where he's Christopher Plummer and I'm Julie Andrews and we're dancing on the marble floor of an Austrian terrace garden. Somehow my head presses Nick's T-shirt and in this moment I am forgetting about time and Tal because maybe my life isn't over. Maybe it's only beginning.

I shiver at that thought and in response, Nick takes his jacket off and places it around my shoulders. I feel safe and not cold and from the vibe the jacket gives off, I also feel fairly confident that the original Texaco Salvatore was a good family man, with perhaps a propensity for wearing his wife's panties and betting his kids' college money at the track, but otherwise a solid dude.

I wake up from the dance dream when the audience applauds the end of the stage performance and Nick feels pressed too close against me without the music going. Nick/Salvatore/Christopher Plummer/lovely dancing-partner man can't be real. It's not possible. Better to end this dream before it becomes a nightmare.

"Why are you so fucking *nice*?" I ask, and shove Nick away. I don't bother to acknowledge his shocked expression. Score, Norah. I have killed his smile, and I didn't even have to tell him about Tris. "I gotta pee."

I run away, toward the bathroom. A few people are waiting at the door but a single finger snap from Toni and the line disperses.

I don't really have to pee. I need to think. I need to sleep. I need Caroline to be sober so I can talk to her. This morning, my life seemed so clear. Turn down Brown, check. Go into the city to see the band Caroline likes rather than suffer through an evening with Mom and Dad entertaining the dreaded hip-hop people at the house, check. This night was supposed to end like any other night out with Caroline—watch her hook up with a guy, then get her home safely. Check. I'm not that girl who randomly meets a guy one night and has her life change. I wear cords and flannel shirts. I don't have the killer body like Tris or Caroline. Sometimes I don't wash my hair for three days and sometimes I don't floss. What's this Nick guy doing here with me?

I step inside the bathroom as the previous occupant leaves. I clean the toilet with a paper towel, then sit down on it. A trail of graffiti is written down the wall next to the toilet.

Jimmy gives good head. Climb Ev'ry Mountain, indeed. (Illustrated.)

Happiness serves hardly any other purpose than to make unhappiness possible.—Proust

You're the one for me, fatty.—Morrissey

I want it that way.—Backstreet Boys (Also illustrated, much more lewd than the Jimmy picture, and finer drawing skills.)

Claire, meet me on Rivington in front of the candy store after the show. You bring the Pez. You know.

Psst—Sitting on the john and wondering when this night will end? Answer: NEVER. Where's Fluffy, unannounced show, TONIGHT, after the von Trapp massacre, before dawn rises. Be there or be square, ayyyy . . . . . .

There's no date written on the wall but the black-marker handwriting looks fresh. I'm curious whose executive decision it was to name the toilet "the john," anyway? But could this show be tonight? I only fucking worship Where's Fluffy. They turned down Dad to sign up with Uncle Lou's indie label. They could make me pogo-stick dance all night. They could make me forget I want to crawl into my bed and hide under the covers, and that I only wasted my youth on Tal, and that I'm on a date with a good guy and I've given him more mixed signals than a dyslexic Morse code operator.

Do I dare show my face back at the table to Nick, tell him about Where's Fluffy? I know he's a fan. I swiped the last make-up mix he burned for Tris that led off with the Where's Fluffy track, "Take Me Back, Bitch." God, he made great playlists for her. Tal's mixes for me were all Dylan and Yma Sumac crap. Nick could mix Cesaria Evora to Wilco to Ani followed by Rancid, capped off with Patsy Cline blending into a Fugazi finale. Although at some point, if our whatever-it-is-happening-this-night progresses, I'll have to reeducate Nick on the poor use of Patti Smith and Velvet Underground tracks on lovesick playlists. Fucking hate them. Patti Smith was a poser suck-up, and Lou Reed was just a plain dick.

DICK! Did I really ask Nick if he had a name for his dick?

Maybe Tal called it right—I should have been more grateful for him, because no guy besides Tal would ever put up with me.

Caroline may be passed out in a stranger's van right now,

but I know what she would say to me now: "Tal was NOT right. And go back out there and give this a better shot. You can do this. Bitch, get the fuck back out there."

I pick up the black Sharpie pen dangling from a string attached to the bathroom mirror and scribble my contribution to the graffiti trail on the wall:

The Cure. For the Ex's? I'm sorry, Nick. You know. Will you kiss me again?

I splash some cold water on my face at the bathroom sink and take a deep breath. Time to go back out there and make this right. I am brand-new. I can change. Only not for Tal. For me.

7. NICK

I am doing everything right. And it is getting the exact right reaction. This is like a miracle to me.

I am as intimidated as fuck to be in the VIP section. I am a little mesmerized by the left nun, who is actually playing the acoustic guitar for "Edelweiss" and twirling her pasties at the same time. I am afraid of the way Norah's looking at me like I have a chance. But somehow I manage to step out of my seat and get her to step out of her seat. I know exactly where to put my hands and where to put her body and just like that we are locked together in a moment, and it is, remarkably, the exact right thing for the moment to be.

I am not used to this.

I don't even notice when the music ends, I am so in my own music. But then the record scratches, the DJ bobbles, the moment crashes, the right turns wrong, Norah pushes me away and spits the word *nice* out at me, then runs to pee.

I am not used to this, either. But I expect it more.

I watch as she goes. Tony/Toni/Toné acts as her fairy godmotherfather, waving a Playboy Bunny air freshener in the air to part the crowd around the Laydies' Room (as opposed to the Laddies' Room, which seems, from the exasperated looks of the people on line, to be currently occupied by a Tantric pair). The nuns on stage have now broken all of their habits, and are parading around in sprigs of what I can only imagine is edelweiss. I can see a lonely goatherd gawking from the front row.

This should divert me, but my mind keeps returning to a simple, scary fact:

I am liking Norah.

I am liking the way she's friends with Playboygirl Bunnies. I am liking the way she knows how to drive stick. I am liking that I have to earn her smiles and laughs. I am liking the way she kissed me. I am liking the way she seems to be able to get past the past. I could learn from that. I am liking that I can throw any kind of sentence at her without worrying it's too out there.

I could easily start to obsess (or, at least, stress) about this, but luckily another diversion soon joins me at the table. It's Tony/Toni/Toné, dressed now as a priest. I mean, he's dressed as a woman dressed as a priest.

"I'm on in ten minutes," she says, to explain the costume change. "Is Norah still powdering?"

"She's the lulu of the loo."

"Perfect! Now us girls can chat." She bows her head in my direction, ready to listen, but even readier to ask. "How long have the two of you been the two of you?"

I look at my watch. "About an hour, including transportation."

Tony/Toni/Toné whistles her appreciation. "That's four times as long as any of *my* relationships have lasted."

"Well, this one might not be setting any new world records," I find myself saying.

"No!" Tony/Toni/Toné exclaims. "I saw the two of you canoodling. You're a regular Johnny Castle."

I have no idea who Johnny Castle is, but I definitely approve of the name.

Tony/Toni/Toné places her palms together and looks at me with a kindness that has no sexuality. "Do you want to talk about it?"

"Yes. No. I don't know."

"How long has it been since your last confession?"

I look him right back in the eye and answer.

"Three weeks, two days, and twenty-four—fuck. Three weeks and three days ago, I guess."

"And what was that confession?"

" 'I love you.' "

"That's a serious one. And how was it received?"

"Vow of silence. And chastity, until the next guy came along."

"So what do you have to confess now?"

I don't know why I'm saying any of this, except that it's the truth.

"I'm confessing that I don't know if I'm ready for this."

"What is 'this'?"

Being open. Being hurt. Liking. Not being liked. Seeing the flicker on. Seeing the flicker off. Leaping. Falling. Crashing.

"Norah. I don't know if I'm ready for Norah."

Tony/Toni/Toné smiles, her teeth the same white as her collar.

"There's no such thing as ready," she says. "There's only willing."

She reaches over and puts her hand on top of mine. She's not making a pass at me—she's trying to pass something on.

"I have all the proof I need," she says. "The proof is always in the dancing."

Her glance escapes from me for a second. I follow it and see Norah emerging from the Laydies' Room.

Tony/Toni/Toné stands up from her chair.

"One more thing?" I ask her.

She raises an eyebrow.

"Who's Norah's dad?"

The eyebrow slants higher, so it's practically perpendicular to her eye.

"You really don't know?" she asks.

I shake my head.

"That," she says, "is brilliant."

Norah isn't looking over to the table—not looking over to me, I figure. She doesn't see Tony/Toni/Toné slip away backstage. She doesn't see me waiting for her.

I decide to check my wallet, to make sure I have enough money to pay for our cocktease cocktails (virginity sullied only by the umbrella's reputation). But of course when she gets to the table, it looks like I'm itching to pay the bill. I quickly shove my wallet back in my pocket, only it gets tangled on its own chain and I end up spewing Washingtons all over the floor. I swoop them up before she sits down again, which only bumps me slightly lower on the spaz scale. Especially because it's now I remember we're being comped, so I didn't have to take my wallet out in the first place.

She seems a little less rattled now.

"You look refreshed," I tell her. Then I can't help myself, adding, "Everything okay? Was it something I said? Or was my Johnny Castle impression just no good?"

She twinkles at Johnny Castle.

Thank you, Tony/Toni/Toné.

"Look," she says, raising her Tina Colada, "I owe you a kind of explanation. I know you probably think I'm a horrid bitch from the planet Schizophrenia, but I'm honestly not trying to mess with your head. I'm just messing with my own head and I seem to have dragged you along for the ride. I think you're nice to me and that scares the fuck out of me. Because when a guy's a jerk or an asshole, it's easier because you know exactly where you stand. Since trust isn't an option, you don't have to get all freaked out about maybe having to trust him. Right now I am thinking about ten things at the same time, and at least four of those things have to do with you. If you want to leave right now and drive home and forget my name and forget what I look like, I wouldn't blame you in the least. But what I'm trying to say is that if you did that I would be sorry. And not just sorry in an I-apologize-I'm-so-sorry way, but sorry in a sad-that-something-that-could've-happened-didn't way. That's it. You can go now. Or we could stay for Where's Fluffy when Toni's set is over. I think they're playing a surprise show here tonight."

Then, finally, she takes a sip of her drink.

A gulp, really.

And I take a deep breath. And I say:

"My jacket looks good on you."

She puts the glass down. Stares at me. And I think, *Fine, I'm a freak.*

So be it.

"No," I go on. "It does. And if I left, you'd probably want to give me my jacket back. And if you did, I wouldn't be able to put it on, because the whole time I'd be knowing how perfectly it fit on you. How even though the sleeves are ridiculously too long and the collar is all fucked up and for all I know some guy named Salvatore is going to come in this very club in two minutes and say, 'Hey, that's my jacket' and strike up a conversation and sweep you off your feet away from me—even though all those things are true or possibly true, I just can't ruin the picture of you sitting there across from me wearing my jacket better than I or anyone else ever could. If I don't owe it to you and I don't owe it to me, I at least owe it to Salvatore."

There. I've said everything I wanted to say without actually having to use the words *please stay.*

"Pick up your drink," Norah tells me.

I do.

She clinks her glass against mine.

"Cheers," she says.

"Salud," I reply.

"L'chaim."

"Top o' the morning to ya."

"Sto lat."

"May the road rise to meet you."

. . . and we go on like this, until Tony/Toni/Toné appears onstage to purr the filthiest "Do Re Mi" that Manhattan has ever seen.

People look at us every now and then. I guess some of them know Norah, or at least who she is. I'm the mystery. Or maybe I'm just the nobody. I don't care. If I'm just The Guy With Norah, that's cool. Right now, that's all I want to be.

All the other things I am—they're too complicated. I can feel them lying in wait, planning their return.

8. NORAH

"So say we're at the Motel 6 on the other side of the Lincoln Tunnel and we're having that threeway with E.T. Who gets to be the top and who gets to be the bottom?"

This question has actually escaped my mouth. Perhaps it's not that I'm frigid—it's that once I decide I like a guy, I turn into a raging idiot, unfit for public appearances. I wish Caroline could be here now, hiding out in a corner, feeding me lines, Cyrano to Nick's Roxanne. Although Caroline-as-inspiration could easily land me right back in the bathroom, on my knees, and not in prayer. Which as a basic premise isn't so objectionable, but now that I'm trying to get in sync with time, I need more of it than Caroline generally requires to reach room temperature with a guy.

Nick answers, "No-brainer. E.T. can't take the heat and goes off to the motel vending machine for some Reese's Pieces, and hopefully doesn't get caught in the crossfire of some crack deal gone bad while he's out there. I mean, really, Norah, Motel 6 off the tunnel? Couldn't we class it up a little? Wouldn't the devirginization of E.T. merit at least a Radisson, at least Paramus?"

The stage acts are over and nuns have converted to stagehands as they transform the set for the next show. We've hit the jackpot, because the Where's Fluffy unannounced show is most certainly going on next after the stage is converted—widened, barricaded, made ready for the coming apocalypse sure to be wrought by the leathered and chained, tunneled, tattooed, and pierced punk crowd now streaming into this place. It's got to be close to three in the morning, because it's the die-hard wave coming in, amped from a night of power-punk club-hopping, ready for the ultimate nightcap. By all logic, I should be home now, sitting up in my twin bed and flicking through channels in the dark while Caroline heaves through her inebriated slumber in her bed across from me. I recognize several people that were at Crazy Lou's earlier, and I know we're all following the same yellow brick road, looking for that ultimate band, that ultimate night to remember. Crazy Lou himself has even arrived, I can see him at the bar chatting up Toni. I can only pray hard that Toni's almighty powers extend to her denying Tal entrance should he follow Lou here tonight, or that Tal will be too jet-lagged for the infinite Manhattan night.

Or maybe prayer isn't necessary and my moment of clarity was real and true and Tal is not a threat because I am wearing this jacket that says Salvatore and I am deep into this night with this Nick person and I am having occasionally really, truly pornographic thoughts about him. While Tal may not yet have wholly receded to the farthest reaches of my subconscious past—I can feel the present bitter taste of his nearness despite the sweetness of the Tina Colada I am drinking—I am here and I am now and there's nowhere I'd rather be, only where did Nick go?

He said I wear his jacket better than he or anyone else ever could. So why isn't he going for an encore Johnny Castle performance with me instead of sitting opposite me acting all casual, looking perhaps a little distracted? He could at least do me the courtesy of trying for some furtive cleavage views, or if nothing else, pretend that he's as interested in learning as much about me as I'd like to know about him. Like, *everything*. Like, *NOW*.

If Caroline was here, she'd give me her *Patience, grasshopper* speech. But she's not and I am left to wonder on my own: How does this work, the getting to know a new guy without revealing too much desperation for his undivided attention?

It helps that the club has gone from full to packed, because the energy and noise help drown out what is fast becoming a sinking ship between Nick and me, probably courtesy of me and the trying-too-hard conversation. I came back from the bathroom, we had virgin drinks along with toasted clinks, but I seem to have made the ultimate mistake. I try to learn something about him (isn't that what you do?), dig a little deeper, and I'm getting sucked down fast into the vortex of Awkward First Date.

"So, where do you live?" I ask him, even though I know. Just to say something. And because E.T. tanked, and *How long have you been in a band?* and *Are you guys serious or just fucking around?* got me only *Since the dawn of time* and *No, we've only been rehearsing together since freshman year, spent every fucking dollar we made at minimum-wage jobs to support this band, but no, we're not fucking serious*. I'm all for sarcasm but sometimes it's tiring, especially when it's near morning and I thought we were finally getting somewhere and I might as well be taking a nap at this point. Nick was so with me a while ago, but now without the diversion of a stage show, and with the (I think) mutual admittance of a mutual . . . *something,* it's like the pendulum is swinging perilously in the wrong direction for us, and I don't know if it's that something changed, or I said something stupid again (fucking E.T.—I HATE you!), or I just dared to fly too close to the sun in my desire to thaw.

"I live in Hoboken," Nick mumbles, and I am remembering a Sinatra-centric mix he made for Tris that made me so hot with envy of her that I wouldn't let her copy my Latin test answers that day.

"College?" I ask him.

"Haven't figured that one out yet."

Brick. Fucking. Wall.

This is why I should consider breaking my straight-edge vow. Beer most certainly would help this situation. It probably couldn't make it any worse.

Basic quiz-show format isn't working here, so I take inspiration from the divine beings that have performed on this stage this evening. I sing this next question, all fake Julie Andrews shit operetta stylee: "Care to name a few of your favorite things?"

His half smile creeps back. "Ben & Jerry's Chubby Hubby ice cream, original Tiffany stained-glass windows at random houses in Weehawken, my iPod. A hot-oil massage from Reba McIntyre."

I rest my case.

Did DJ Irony *plan* to spin "Heaven Knows I'm Miserable Now" by The Smiths right now to appease the crowd during the interim stage setup between acts, or is it just coincidence?

What did I miss? What changed?

I take one last shot. Come back to Mama, Nick. You can do it.

"Last moment of true happiness you experienced?" I ask him.

"Sometime before three weeks, three days ago . . ."

And he's gone again. Ohhhhh . . . .

The air is hot here from the surge of people coming in and I watch him watching the door and I realize he's scared Tris is going to show. She probably will. An underground band about to hit it big performing in the middle of the night for a secret show, surely there's an almost-famous musician about to come onstage looking for some groupie Tris love.

I feel for Nick. He doesn't know yet that he'll be okay without her. Part of me wonders if I should even bother here. The other part of me wants to scream at him: *What did you see in her? Why did you waste your life on her?*

Only I already know the answers to the Tris quiz show. If I can suck it up enough to look past the obvious—the blond hair, the big tits, the long legs, the tight skirts—I know that there's this other Tris, this girl who can show a guy a good time without the Caroline variety hangover, make him feel wanted and special until her attention inevitably wanes, this girl who will kick ass at FIT next year, this girl who will have your back, no questions asked.

In Nick's absence of words and his vacant look, I am remembering junior year in the bathroom, after I'd tanked on a Bio exam. I was drying my hands with a paper towel when Tris came from behind me and snatched the paper towel away from me. "You realize you've been drying your hands for about three straight minutes now? You've practically parched your skin. You okay?" And just like that I came out with it: "I'm late." "You're paranoid," Caroline had said when I told her, while Tal had said, "Don't you dare make any decisions without consulting me first." But it was Tris who grabbed my arm and said, "C'mon." It was Tris who knew the strictly Jersey public bus that could take us to the nearby CVS and not to the city, Tris who waited outside the bathroom for me at Starbucks while I took the test, Tris who shoved me in the chest afterward and said, "Be more careful next time, bitch." It was Tris who stood in line to buy me a Frappuccino with her back to me after, knowing I wouldn't want her to see me cry. And I know we really don't like each other except for having known each other since elementary school and the whole past and shared childhood of that, and I know she is a lying cheating skank because how could she do what she did to this guy?; but I also know there is like some girl code I should be obeying and not treading into new dangerous territory with her castoff, so maybe that's why it's Nick who's suddenly gone all frigid?

The Smiths song ends, to a smattering of applause coming

from the direction of the bathrooms. The cocktail bunny has responded to the urgent calls of nature of a long line of laddies waiting for the loo and unlocked the bathroom door with the key hanging from the chain around her neck. Even with the dank lighting and through the beads separating the bathroom area from the club, it's clear that it's Hunter wrapped inside the arms of the singer for Nick's band, I think his name was Dev. They're standing against the red wall, locked in one of those deep, soul-enjoined kisses that can only cause observers of the kiss to have a crisis of deep, soul-searching envy.

Nick finally laughs again, and my heart tries not to leap. "That's our Dev!"

As their mouths disengage, Dev plucks a strand of hair from Hunter's face and twirls it through his fingers. With his other hand, Dev waves hello to the exasperated line of laddies.

I point out, "Damn, even from here, you can see the smile on his face."

"Dev's the reason our band doesn't have a drummer."

"How's that?" We're going again. Thank you, Dev, you stud, thank you.

"We used to have a great drummer. The guy killed, he was so good. Then Dev 'turned' him. The dude didn't even know he liked boys before—"

"Oh, he knew." Because they always do, whether or not they'll admit it.

Nick shrugs. "Could be. But Dev brought him out. And once the closet door had swung wide open, the poor guy wanted a boyfriend. Dev had just wanted a conquest. Especially one who had been the All-American high school track star."

"Dev is a slut?"

"That's our boy."

Dev's trailing Hunter by the hand now, and they are snaking their way through the club. Their performance has merited the offering of two coveted barstools from the packed bar area. The dynamic duo take these offerings and haul them over to our table and sit themselves down.

"Nice show," I tell Dev.

"Wasn't it?" Dev laughs. He looks like the love child of a Bollywood movie star and whoever this year's Adam Brody is. I can't blame Hunter, or the M.I.A. drummer. Dev's a fucking babe, whose point score doesn't even receive deductions for the faded and torn "Lodi Track & Field" shirt he's wearing.

Dev's animation is the antithesis of casual-boy Nick. "FUCK! You heard about the show? Where's Fluffy! WHERE'S FUCKING FLUFFY!" He plays mock drums on the table and Nick lifts his eyebrow at me and gives me a knowing smile and for a flash lightning stroke of a moment, I suspect the time-out is ending and we might be getting back in the game.

And then our ref sashays to our table like the beauty queen s/he is and addresses Nick like they're old sorority sisters: "Girl, be a dear and help me with some of this stage equipment, will you?" Nick jumps to his feet like he's been waiting for Toni's salvation all along. Good—maybe Toni can share some PMS elixir with Nick and send him back revived.

"WHERE'S FLUFFY!" Dev shouts. He pats my back in excitement then raises his arms like he's Rocky. "WHERE'S FUCKING FLUFFY!"

Exactly. This was the reaction I expected from Nick when I told him about the show. I mean, they're only the best punk band out there right now, named for the fucking apathy of a xenophobic fucking nation oblivious to the fucking terror its leaders wreak on the rest of the world because they're too busy worrying if their cat might be stuck up a tree or something. Where's Fluffy can actually play instead of just wail like fucking pop-punk goof-offs. They sing everything right about everything wrong—they'll come on pro-NRA, anti-choice, homophobic—to remind listeners what's worth fighting for. Where's Fluffy are the real deal, and if there is anything between me and Nick, it will be determined when the show starts, if we're front and center in jumping throttling exhilaration together, fist-waving and shouting "oi oi oi" at all the right moments, in sync. So to speak.

The mosh pit will reveal all the answers. The mosh pit never lies.

9. NICK

Things are going so well. We're volleying words back and forth. Everything she says, I have something I can say back. We're sparking, and part of me just wants to sit back and watch. We're clicking. Not because a part of me is fitting into a part of her. But because our words are clicking into each other to form sentences and our sentences are clicking into each other to form dialogue and our dialogue is clicking together to form this scene from this ongoing movie that's as comfortable as it is unrehearsed.

I know she's holding back a little. I know she keeps shooting me questions so I won't get too close to her answers. That's fine. Who is she, really? Fuck if I know. But I care. Yeah, I'm starting to care.

The club is really packed now, filled with that pre-gig mix of anticipation and extreme impatience. Dev is so completely Dev and ramps himself over to us to lead the WHERE THE FUCK IS FLUFFY? cheer. Tony/i/é comes over and wants me to help with some gear. I look at Norah and almost ask if she's going to miss me while I'm gone. But I don't want to push it.

It's pretty cool to be in the realm of Fluffy, even if I can't see any of the guys and all I'm doing is making sure the mics work. Just to be standing on their stage is a bit of a rush. I'm testing 1-2-3 and testing FUCK-SHIT-COCK and the crowd is looking at me with this unanimous wish that I'd get the fuck off the stage, and if it wasn't for the presence of a glowering man in Playboy Bunny pose watching over me, I might be having some head-meet-bottle moments. And it would almost be worth it. It's not often that you can shed blood for one of your favorite bands.

It's all so fucking surreal. And suddenly I'm wanting to tell Tris about it. Which is so fucking wrong, but it's not the kind of thought that's a choice. Where's Fluffy was the second show we went to, and the sixth, and the eleventh, and the fourteenth. She'd never heard of them, so I dragged her well past midnight to see them at Maxwell's, underage but not underambitious. She was so skeptical of bands she'd never heard of—like she couldn't get a buzz if there hadn't been some buzz. Where's Fluffy convinced her, though. She got it on the first song and wasn't afraid to show it. She whooped and hacksawed and knifed up and hair-flailed nonstop for the full 110 rpm set. Afterward she said, "Man, those guys were hot," and I was so entirely jealous of them, until she said, "But not as hot as you right now" and I became a firework waiting to happen.

But that wasn't all. I'm thinking about the sixth time. I was dancing, doing my thing, and she just stopped for a moment, looking at me. And I screamed, "What?" and she screamed back, "You have to stop that," and I screamed "What?" and she told me, "You're still here. You have to go farther than that." And at first I didn't get it, but then I realized that she was right; I wasn't giving myself up to the music. I was looking at the people around me. I was self-conscious. I was contexting every single note. "Just let go," she yelled. And at first I couldn't, since I was so grounded in the trying. But then the band launched into "Dead Voter" and for the first time ever I freed myself from everything but the chords. I didn't think about Tris—she had hidden herself behind the song, orchestrating it all. After we were done, sweat-glazed and panting, we didn't have to say a fucking word. We just looked at each other and there was this recognition. She'd pushed me and I'd gotten there. I was grateful. Am grateful.

I look at the crowd for a moment, trying to find her again. I know she's there somewhere, even if she's not in the room. Even if she's making out with some other guy in some other club without one single synapse connecting a thought of me.

"Wake the fuck up!" some guy pressing against the stage says. I realize that my hands have fallen idle. Like I can't think of Tris and do anything else at the same time. Which is such a lie.

I finish the connections. The mics are ready for the assault. Tony/i/é nods and the lights dim. I head off, but not before I catch the nod of Evan E., Fluffy's drummer. I smile and nod back, then press back into the crowd. I've lost track of Norah, lost sight of where our table used to be. All the tables have been shoved aside now.

Fuse: lit.

Fuse: burning.

Ready.

Set.

Explode.

The guitars rampage. The drums batter. Owen O. snarls bastardizations at the world. A bell rings and Pavlov's dog has a fucking seizure on the dance floor. Since I'm not a part of it yet, I see it: how a group of people can become a blizzard, how all the time spent buying and picking out exactly the right clothes doesn't mean shit now because nobody is looking at clothes or poses. It's about force and pulse and unleashing the gigantic urges. I am pushing through skin and spike to get to Norah. I am jolting through this human turbulence to catch sight of Tris. I am slamming though this bright, bright darkness to figure out who the fuck I'm looking for, and why.

Norah. She's ten feet away. Not looking for me or for anything else. She is in the middle of this conflagration and she looks entirely alone.

It scares me.

I recognize it.

I am hearing Lars L.'s bassline. I am falling into it, the black of it, the pit of it. It screams that time is an angry machine. Music is an angry machine. We are all angry machines.

I've lost my kilter. I am downwarding. And it's worse because I know I should be going up.

Norah. Just make your way to Norah.

Dev is in my way. I try to maneuver around him, and he responds with a fevered shove. I shove back. He catches my shoulder too hard and I spin out. I stumble. I bodycheck Norah.

She doesn't laugh. She just throws herself right back at me. Slam and retreat. Then *I* slam and retreat. We should be smiling and we're not smiling. I throw my whole body at her, full-frontal crash. She is all resistance. She holds her ground and there we are, no distance now, her face so close it's almost a blur.

"What the fuck?" she yells, and it's not me she's speaking to.

Dev's elbow hits my back and I press forward and she's right there and I'm reaching out and she's right there and right at that moment the amps amplify and the music takes on such a pulse that it becomes my heartbeat and her heartbeat and I know it and she knows it and this is the point where we could break apart and that would be it, totally it. But I look into her eyes and she looks into my eyes and we recognize it—the excitement of being here, the excitement of being now. And maybe I'm realizing what a part of it she is and maybe she's realizing what a part of it I am, because suddenly we're not crashing as much as we're combining. The chords swirling around us are becoming a tornado, tightening and tightening and tightening, and we are at the center of it, and we are at the center of each other. My wrist touches hers right at the point of our pulses, and I swear I can feel it. That thrum. We are moving to the music and at the same time we are a stillness. I am not losing myself in the barrage. I am finding her. And she is—yes, she is finding me. The crowd is pressing in on us and the bassline is revealing everything and we are two people who are part of a lot more people, and at the same time we're our own part. There isn't loneliness, only this intense twoliness. There's only one way to test it, and that is to dare a movement, to push it farther and see if she wants it to go there. I find her lips and I make that kiss and she's pulling my hair and I've got the fabric of her jacket bunched in a fist and it's nothing like talking and it's right there and we're taking it and taking it and taking it. And my eyes are closed and then my eyes are open and I see her eyes are open and there's a part of her that's pulling back even as our bodies are pressing and it's the fear, of course there's the fear, and I just hold her close to tell her I understand.

Lars L. launches straight into "Take Me Back, Bitch" and I flinch and Norah sees it and I have no way of saying it's not her, it's not now, it's the ten thousand thens that she has nothing to do with. I lean in and kiss her again, the same way that you run to your room and blast the music when your parents start shouting. I know it won't work and it doesn't work because some things you don't need to hear in order to hear. The mind has an ear of its own and sometimes memory is the fiercest fucking DJ alive.

Now Norah's yelling "What?" and it *is* a question for me. And then she says the hardest question of all—the one that takes so much hurt and bravery to ask—which is "Why did you stop?" and the bassline is too strong and my body is being battered from all sides and one of my favorite bands has turned against me and I'm yelling "I CAN'T TALK TO YOU HERE" and she screams "WHAT?" and I am right in her ear and yell "NOT HERE" and then "I CAN'T TALK."

Her hand finds my hand and immediately I'm being led away. We are piercing through the rumbling tumbling crowd and our arms are like the most precarious bridge, held together by that single, pulling clasp. I think, *If she lets go, it's all over. If I let go, it's all over.* And because she is holding on so tight, I hold on so tight. I am being jostled from all sides—I know there will be bruises tomorrow—but somehow this hand-hold is immune. Somehow we stay together. We are graced, and we are together, and the twoliness is trumping the loneliness and the doubt and the fear. We are making it through. Thank you, music. Damn you, memories. Thank you, present.

She looks around, then gets me into a small room to the side of the Laddies' Room. It's the size of a closet, and it's dominated by a lime-green couch in front of a big mirror. There's a priest's collar thrown over the back of the couch, and plenty of open makeup. I expect Norah to look at me mischievously, but instead she looks determined. She keeps hold of my hand and launches herself into me, squeezing and grappling and kissing me so hard my lips can barely kiss back.

"You," she says, her hand now leading my hand over her breasts and her free hand gliding over my chest. And it's hot in this small room, and she's feverish and she's kissing me and my mouth is opening and her hands, her tongue, her hips are exploring. But her eyes aren't as adventurous. And I don't know if she's trying to pull me back or pull me in or just plain trying to pull. If this is desire, I'm not clear what it's a desire for. I'm aroused—so fucking aroused—by the heat of it, the fever of it, the dark—yes, darkness—of it. But I can't lose myself in it because I can't find where she is, outside of the music, inside these movements. Her hand is pressing my hand against the wall, and the other hand is under my shirt, rising up to my neck, then starting to go back down. And down. And her fingers have found my trail and my hands both press the wall. The heat of it, the fever of it . . . the look in her eyes is unsmiling and I just want it and I just can't do it and she's reaching down and down and as she touches me there I am about to explode and I want her to say something, even my name, but she doesn't and suddenly I can't. I want to be sure, and I'm not sure, and I say no, because I want her to be sure and I just can't be sure that she is. She kisses me again and strokes a little and this time I'm really not kissing back and I've got to stop it before something happens and I don't understand what's going on here and I let go of her hand and her other hand stops and even though I am up against a wall, I pull away.

Why did you stop?

I don't want her to say it. But it's there in her face. If she had something to prove, now I've disproven it. So the dead equation of our actions lies between us, and I don't know what the fuck I can do.

"Did you see her?" she asks. And at first I want to ask who. But then I know, and I say no, and I ask, "Did you see him?"

She turns ten degrees away from me, back toward the noise, and answers yes.

10. NORAH

The mosh pit didn't lie. I knew that and yet I ignored the evidence the pit threw back at me. *Why did you stop?* Can the oracle answer the one better question now: *Why the fuck did I keep going?*

I tell Nick, "Yes." He thinks I mean, Yes, I saw Tal. I didn't see Tal. I did see Tris. It will be easier for Nick, later, if he thinks it's Tal I saw. Then he can blame it all on me and my hang-ups. But there's a reason women go frigid and Nick can fucking go look in the mirror if he wants to view that reason.

WHY AM I SUCH A FUCKING LOSER?

I race out of the closet room, slamming the door behind me with my foot, pleased by the snarl of "OW, THAT FUCKING HURT!" I hear from Nick's side of the door. I know Nick needs a few minutes to himself to get his parts back in order. I have some time to do what I need to do.

What I did not need to do was what I just did. I got no Oi. I only got Oy. I trusted in the power of the pit, believed in the come-on when Nick tested FUCK-SHIT-COCK on the mic, looking right at me. I knew there was no way Tris would not be showing up at this club, and knew I'd better take my chance before it blew up like Where's Fluffy in performance. I've never been the girl to make a move, which is maybe why night after night I go out with Caroline and the moves are always made on her but never on me. And I wasn't thinking about Where's Fluffy opening their set with "Take Me Back, Bitch" when I did what I did, moved what I moved. I was thinking about that second song on the playlist Nick made for Tris, "Take a Chance on Me" by Abba. Either Dev slipped something into my Tina Colada or it was the sensual memory of the song of the Swedes, because I was in the pit with Dev and Hunter and I was believing in the band and in time and in the mosh, maybe even believing in God and Nick. That heaven-hell was hot as fuck in the middle, and that had to be the sign that I needed to just fucking go for it.

First shot at bat? Strikeout. All wrong. My eyes were open for the second half of that horrible-great kiss and right on schedule I saw Toni frisking Tris at the door and I knew my window of opportunity was about to slam shit, I mean shut. I am nothing if not determined, as well as extremely foolish, so it was not my hormones leading Nick to the closet room for a second shit, I mean shot; no, it was worse, it was plain stupidity leading me, the patented Norah-brand stupidity (the kind that writes regression letters to Evil Exes) that my brain holds in higher contempt than ignorance because it's the exclusive Norah brand that will lead down a path to what I hate most: regret.

I didn't even bother with foreplay, I lunged right in like I was Tal after too much Manischewitz Passover wine. I knew it was too soon, Nick was too raw, but I was goddamn ready to thaw and prove I wouldn't leave him cold. And I thought I did prove that, I mean I had him, at least I thought I did, I mean he responded, sort of, at least I thought he did, or maybe what I thought was response and mutual attraction was merely the fact that he's a guy, and an Elmo doll could accidentally graze it and it would respond. But the moment passed so quickly and if I am being honest, I know it only half responded and barely that because Julio probably knew it was Sub Z calling.

I will not do any more instant replay of that scene. I will not.

I am so humiliated.

I can feel the humiliation burning my face, branding me, making me hotter than frigid could ever imagine being, hot with hate. I hate the regret, pumping through every artery of my body, craving a cheeseburger right now. I hate time and I hate this night and if I truly believed in God outside of that momentary lapse of faith, I'd hate Her too.

I even hate Where's Fluffy. My former favorite band, now destined to be remembered for the rest of my life as the band I was listening to when I went down like the *Titanic,* ahem. I hate Caroline for being passed out when I really need to talk to her. I hate Tal for all the times of *No, touch it this way* and *You're doing it all wrong, Norah,* because now Nick, my first shot at redemption, knows it too: I have no fucking idea how to do this. It's like that mythic God takes human beings at creation and divides us into subsets: Group A gets the hot looks, sex appeal, and lots of action with natural ease (Caroline); Group B is the makeover prospects who will figure it all out and eventually get their action (Tris); and Group C is the rest of the poor schmucks (me) for whom God has decided, *You're on your own. Don't expect much.*

I kind of hate Nick right now, too, but there's someone else higher on my list, someone I hate more than Saddam Hussein and any asshole named Bush combined, hate more than that fuckhead who canceled *My So-Called Life* and left me with a too-small boxed DVD set that does not answer the questions of whether Angela and Jordan Catalano ever did it, or if Patty and Graham got a divorce, or if there really was something to all that lesbian subtext between Rayanne and Sharon. I need to fucking find that person I hate most, so I can hopefully at least kill that other hate, the one called regret.

The crowd is surging toward the pit. The band is between songs and an inconceivable lull is taking place onstage while Lars L. gets in tune and adjusts the mic against the feedback Nick probably fucked up when he tried to help Toni with set-up. Lars L. knows the potential of the crowd to turn against the band if given even a moment of silence and he must be noticing the crowd surge because he shouts at the audience, "What the fuck should we play next?" and a mohawked punk at the top yells, "Just play fucking something!" and the punk hasn't even finished the statement before Evan E. yells out ONE-TWO-THREE-FOUR as he drumbangs, and in a psychedelic flash Owen O. is raging out Where's Fluffy's cover of the gospel song "I'm Living on God's LSD." For a moment I forget about hate because my body has to thrash to this divine intervention of sound. For one minute of that two-minute song, I am lost to hate because I am lost to Owen O. and Evan E. and Lars L. because they are G. Gods, and everyone here knows it, feels it, shares it.

But then I see the fists waving in the pit and I hear the Oi's and I see a live person being passed around on the extended arms of the crowd, and even in this poor lighting I couldn't miss the bumblebee colors worn by the queen bee. Tris is the crowd-surfer, taking her shot to get passed to the front of the stage and hopefully be ushered backstage.

And I am back at hate.

I part that crowd like I'm fucking Moses, I mean seriously, I am like a five-star general, Commander Pissed-Off Bitch in her own personal marine tank, hurtling through the desert and no one better fucking get in my way. I am in the middle of the mosh within seconds and when it's my turn to propel Tris forward to the stage, instead of letting her legs pass over my upturned palms, I grab for her feet instead and she falls to the ground and the crowd doesn't care, they've gone on to someone else being passed around and Lars L. is pointing at the new victim and nodding YES to the security goons.

Tris stands up from the floor, then holds her hand against her forehead. "THAT FUCKING HURT!" she yells at me and only if she had also snarled "OW!" like Nick could I hate her more right now. I grab her hand from her forehead and lead her through the masses, a stormtrooper with a hostage now. I don't bother to say "bye" to Dev and Hunter, watching us leave from the periphery of the slightly opened eyes of their French kiss.

Once we're outside and I can breathe again, can feel the cold of the early spring-morning air, I am less on hate and more on tired. It's just me and Tris out here, and the smokers and the users against the nearby wall, and it's quiet except for Lars L.'s bassline thumping through the walls and the honking taxis on the street. Finally, I can hear myself, and I am saying, "Why?" to Tris, but actually I'm shouting "WHY?" because my ears haven't yet adjusted to the lower decibel. But already my heart rate is acclimating, slowing down, easing up, released from the suffocation of that club and that noise and so many people inside, who surely all know of my humiliation and my regret.

She's the reason I could not break through to Nick, and I want to know why.

Tris leans against the building wall and rubs her eyes. "I'm so fucking tired," she says. "And you don't fucking have to yell." Caroline is right, that bitch does go pleather, because otherwise no way would Tris mess with a real leather skirt by sliding her ass down the wall and falling to the ground. Tris rests against the building, hugging her knees, her face pressed into her knees.

I sit down next to her. I ask her again, "Why?" and she says, "Nick?" and I say, "Yeah."

She looks like she's going to fall asleep. Her eyes flutter and she almost looks likable, now that she is freed of the club's confines. This is how she is. She'll take you to her personality's farthest reaches of annoying, then manage a late ninth-inning turnaround to being an almost comforting presence.

Caroline and I have known her since Girl Scouts, but she was never a major irritation until high school, after not even the Quakers could tolerate Caroline and I followed Caroline from Friends Country Day to Sacred Heart for junior and senior year. Tris thought our arrival at her school meant the arrival of kindred spirits for her, and she followed us around like a puppy dog, wanting in on our Manhattan music scene. She didn't get that Caroline and I have always strictly been a Gang of Two. Tris thinks she's one of us since she likes the same music and no one at that school would have her, a freak like me and Caroline. We have let her be Two and a Half on occasion; she does have decent radar for good bands, even if odds are she'll make a fool of herself—dancing like a maniac, singing along off-key—whenever we take her along to a music club. But get Tris alone at Starbucks, and she's normal, at least tolerable—she's not laughing too loud, trying too fucking hard. She's my savior with the stick that says negative.

I want to—but I can't—hate her.

She opens one eye at me. "Are you on a fucking date with him or something? Do you like him?"

"Yes," I say, because I don't want to lie, and then "Not really," I amend, because I don't want to lie, and finally, "No," because I don't want to lie. Nick is—was—this thing, this person, I discovered out of nowhere and then discovered I wanted—and once I tasted it, I yearned for it—but I know I must accept defeat because this whole night was an accident, clearly. My heart literally aches, that shit is not made up; it hurts for an unexpected, brief time warp of suddenly wanting and longing and believing, but then not having. Who am

I kidding? The best parts of Nick were ones he doesn't even know I know he has—the lyrics, the playlists, the loyalty—and all of them, dedicated to Tris.

"Did you tell him about me?" she says. Because at school, in the cafeteria, with all the sweet little Catholic girls lined up like plaid dominoes at the tables, and then me, Caroline, and Tris, with our piercings and goth colors and C and T's (but not mine) uniform blouses ordered two sizes too tight, Tris brags about all the guys she dates, the clubs she gets into, the fucking backstage pass of it all, because she wants to impress Caroline. But when it's just the two of us in class, Tris is showing me the mixes Nick made her, the songs he wrote her, the admissions essay he helped her write for FIT.

"No, I didn't tell him," I say. I'm glad I didn't. I didn't want to be the girl trying to know him, but all him knowing of me is what I knew of Tris. "Why did you do it anyway?" I don't know which *why* I want the answer to—why she cheated on him, or why she let him go.

"I'm hungry," Tris states, and I have to agree, "Me too." She stands up, and I take the hand she offers to help lift me up and I don't think this is about a prisoner exchange anymore.

We walk to the 24-hour Korean grocery across the street, and it's like some primal instinct because we both go right to the cookie section and she opens up a bag of Chips Ahoy and I open a bag of Oreos and we are chomping in the aisle, and the owner at the counter is like, "You have to pay for that!" and Tris and I are both like, "WE KNOW!"

She leans her head against a display of Fig Newtons and

says, "It's like this. I met Nick. And I wanted him and I had him but he didn't want to let go, and he was such a fucking great guy, I couldn't let him go, even if there were other guys in the picture." She places her thumb inside her mouth, removing a piece of chocolate chip stuck between her teeth. "But then it got to this point where he's making college choices based on me, thinking we have a future, I mean he's ready to turn down all these great fucking schools to go to Rutgers so he can be near me, and I am thinking, this cannot be happening, he cannot do this. Because he said 'I love you' and, you know, I was just not feeling that back. And I know it must suck to say that and not have the other person say it back, but I felt like now was the time to set him free, so he could find someone else, someone who could say that back to him, because someone *should* say that back to him. I figured it would hurt him much worse later if I had let him believe he had something he didn't, so I took the brutal route. I didn't say 'I love you' back. I said, 'It's over.' I'm eighteen, about to move to the city for school, start my life. I want to have fun. I don't want commitment and 'I love you.'"

She pauses to wolf down another Chips Ahoy. Once she's swallowed it, she says, "Was I like just profound or what?"

Nietzsche fucking Tris may be on to something. Tal told me he loved me, and told me and told me, but you don't tell someone that and then tell them they're not experienced enough in bed and should read a book or something to learn, or they should try wearing deep-red lipstick and tight skirts to look hot like their best friend once in a while. If Tal hadn't lied to me when he said he loved me, I might not be without a future right now, a sucker who was so chickenshit she allowed herself to believe a false dream from a false god. I'm not sure I ever even liked Tal, much less loved him, and by the way, Tal, I believe the Palestinians should have their own state.

For once in my life, I am speechless. I have just eaten my thirteenth consecutive Oreo in under five minutes. When I do speak, I know from the security mirror hanging behind Tris and in front of me that I am speaking from a mouth blackened by Oreo bits. "You have to tell him why, Tris. He deserves to know. And he's gonna be damaged goods until he does know."

So Nick won't be going through my rehabilitation program. That's okay. He'll make some girl, the right girl, a great boyfriend one day. He'll be the love of some lucky girl's life, and maybe after I've had some sleep after this epic night, I'll be glad for him and the future he's waiting to grab, once Tris truly sets him free. So I won't be part of his life other than as this footnote "date." So I have a lifetime of loneliness ahead of me. That's okay, too. There are lots of careers for frigid girls. I can dedicate myself to good deeds. I'll become some U.N. humanitarian (hey, Tal, I fucking believe in the United Nations, too, asshole). I do have two years of Catholic school behind me. I could become a nun even if I am a non-believer. I'll learn to fake it like Nick just did with me. I will minister the gospel of compassion and kindness and please, always use a condom, from famine-stricken nations to war-torn dead zones. It's possible I might become a nun who kisses other nuns—hell, I can look up Becca Weiner from summer camp and see if she wants in on the action—but I know that a few hundred years from now when the post-apocalyptic pope is deciding whether to canonize me, s/he will look the other way on those indiscretions and figure, Hey, Saint Norah was hard up—it happens to all of us. And I will be floating over my heaven-hell dimension, probably in close proximity to my home base Arctic Circle, knowing that the saintly person I became was all because of this night. So I should be thanking Nick, not hating him.

"You're wearing his jacket," Tris says. "He never lets me wear his jacket."

It's Tris whose actions have caused me the night from heaven-hell, so I have no problem letting her pay for my Oreos. I leave her at the counter, fumbling for her wallet. I am ready for home. I am ready to sleep in my own bed, to wake up tomorrow morning and figure out a life plan, and maybe talk to my parents about us all talking to Caroline about getting some fucking help because if we've gotten to the point where Tris is more cool and less scary to hang out with than Caroline, there's obviously a big problem to work out here.

I head for the door, but not before imparting some last saintly wisdom upon Tris. "Be more careful next time, bitch," I tell her.

She doesn't look up from her fumbling wallet maneuver, she just lifts her middle finger with the Jersey-bitch rhinestone-studded black-and-yellow-painted nail tip at me. "Okay, bitch," she calls back to me.

I have enough cash for a cab ride all the way back home and the driver can go fuck himself if he tries to give me grief about a fare to Jersey. I look out onto the street in search of a cab but see Nick instead, leaning against a telephone booth outside the grocery.

I am not about hate anymore, or humiliation, or regret. I'm too tired for that, too done and yet too renewed.

I walk over to him, and mark the sign of the cross from his forehead to his chest to each side of his heart, In the name of the Father, the Son, and the Holy Norah. Then I caress that cheek of Nick's one last time, because I want one last touch, I deserve it. I tell him, "You are absolved."

I walk away, placing my pinkie and index fingers in my mouth to whistle for a cab, all alone on this almost-morning deep in the throes of big bad Lower Manhattan, but protected by the sacred shroud of Salvatore upon mine shoulders.

I'm fucking keeping Nick's jacket.

11. NICK

Fuck her.

Fuck her for getting in that cab. Fuck her for fucking with my mind. Fuck her for not knowing what she wants. Fuck her for dragging me into it. Fuck her for being such a fantastic kisser. Fuck her for ruining my favorite band. Fuck her for barely saying a word to me before she left. Fuck her for not waving. Fuck her for getting my hopes up. Fuck her for making my hopes useless. Fuck her for taking off with my fucking jacket.

Fuck me.

Fuck me for always getting into situations like this. Fuck me for caring. Fuck me for not knowing the words that would've made her stay. Fuck me for *not* knowing what I want. Fuck me for wavering. Fuck me for not kissing her back the right way. Fuck me for getting my hopes up. Fuck me for not having more realistic hopes. Fuck me for giving her my fucking jacket.

Fuck.

If I hadn't stayed those extra two minutes in the dressing room, staring at the mirror, as if my face would suddenly tell me the answers my mind didn't know. If I'd been able to push through the crowd instead of being stuck inside its haphazard body-maze. If I'd seen her in that grocery before she got to the door. If I'd said something when I saw her coming. If I'd managed any of these ifs—would I have been able to avoid the inevitable fuck-up, the full-force fuck-off? My pride shut me up, my hurt shut me down, and together they ganged up on my hope and let her get away.

To go back into the club alone means defeat. To stay outside looking at the taillights of her cab means defeat. To go home and pass out means defeat. To sit right down on the pavement and stare at the curb means defeat—but it's the defeat that's closest, so I sit down and start tracing the edge of the sidewalk. I've moved myself to foot level, which is exactly where I should be. Foot in mouth, stomped all over, kick me kick me kick me. It's Ludlow Street, so the shoes that pass me are all somewhere between hip and porn. Neon-colored sneakers, vixen pumps, stiletto boots for men and women. If I had my guitar, I might be able to make some change. But instead all I have are the songs crashing together in my head. They're all sad. They're all bitter. And they're all that I have.

I didn't let her go. She went. It's not my fault.

She did it.

She could undo it.

This is feeling so fucking familiar.

Why do we even bother? Why do we make ourselves so open to such easy damage? Is it all loneliness? Is it all fear? Or is it just to experience those narcotic moments of belonging with someone else? Norah, don't you know it was as simple as the way you dragged me off the dance floor? You didn't have to make out with me to get me there. And now I know this. And now I can say this. And now you're gone.

It's my fault, isn't it?

Fuck this.

Fuck this wondering. Fuck this trying and trying. Fuck this belief that two people can become one ideal. Fuck this helplessness. Fuck this waiting for something to happen that probably won't ever happen.

"Oh, Nick—what did she do to you?"

Pink Panther–pink open-toed heels. I look up, and it's funny. Because I swear it's Tris standing over me, looking sympathetic. It's like being on one of those TV shows where the dead mother comes back every once in a while to talk. Impossible, but right when you'd most expect her.

"Tris," I say, because I can't think of anything else to say.

She shakes her head, brushes off a spot of pavement, then sits down next to me.

"Where's Norah?" she asks.

I shrug. "Probably three-quarters of the way through the Lincoln Tunnel."

"She never could take it," Tris says, pulling out a cigarette, then handing the lighter to me so I can spark it. "Never. Put her on the spot and she'll just refuse to admit that the spot is there. This one time? We were all going skinny-dipping. No big deal. We all have pools. We know what that's like. But I can tell right away that there's no way Norah's going to do it. This boy she likes—holy shit, I think it was Andy Biggs—well, he's going to be there. And she doesn't want to see him like that. But does she protest? No. Does she put up a fight? No. She comes over with us, plays DJ for a while, and when it's time for us to strip and get in the water, she disappears. Walks like two fucking miles back to her house without saying a word. The next day, she doesn't even pretend she was feeling sick or anything. Doesn't try to explain it at all."

She hasn't said this many words to me in four weeks—no, more than that. Because toward the end all the words started leaving. Except for the ones that had to lock up at the end of the night.

I don't know whether I can touch her. I mean, reach across those two or three inches and let my hand fall on her arm. Feel what that's like again. See if it feels like the past, or something in a different tense.

"Don't," she says. "Don't get fucking moony on me, Nick. Because if you do, I am out of here faster than Norah. Get it?"

I nod. Try not to look at her skin.

"Good." Tris lets loose a smoke signal. "I don't want to talk about us."

You never did, I think.

When someone breaks up with you, their beauty—which you took such satisfaction in—suddenly becomes unfair. It's like that with Tris right now. She's even managed to arrange herself in the lamplight so the shadows hit in just the right way. It feels like a rebuke.

We sit in silence for a second. She takes a drag. She's cinematic and I'm a fucking sitcom. The silence doesn't bother her at all, but it freaks the hell out of me. So I do what

I always vowed not to do, and always found myself doing anyway. I throw "I miss you" into the breach. It even feels empty to me. Like I'm not saying it to the right person.

"Don't start that again," Tris says, but without the edge I was expecting. "It doesn't prove anything except that I don't feel the same way." Another drag of the cigarette, and an ear turned toward the club. "They sound kick-ass tonight, don't they? I thought the big time would ruin them, but maybe I was wrong. I should've slept with Owen O. while I had the chance. Then I would've been only one degree of spread-eration from whatever teen-movie starlet gets to him first. I just hope they don't name their daughter after a fucking fruit."

"April," I say.

"What?"

"April. You said you wanted to name our daughter April."

Tris shoots me a curious look. "Did I? I don't know if it's sweet or scary that you remember that."

I find the courage to ask, "Aren't sweet and scary the same thing to you?"

She grins a little at my insight and nods. "Maybe. Sorry."

"Sorry?"

"Yeah. Sorry."

She draws more of the embers toward her, stares not at me but at the punks walking across the street from us.

"Tris, I—"

"Do you like her?"

"What?"

"Norah. Do you like her?"

"Can you like someone who confuses the hell out of you?"

"All the fucking time."

"Did I confuse the hell out you?"

It's really just a question, but this time Tris *is* annoyed, flicking her cigarette at me so ashes scatter on my shirt.

"Shut up, okay?" she says. "Enough already. ENOUGH. Yes, you confuse the hell out of me. Because not only can you not let go, but you don't even fucking realize that the thing you're holding on to *isn't even there*. You think I hurt you? Well, I could have hurt you so much more."

"How?" I have to ask.

"By *telling the truth,* Nick. I thought you'd see it. I thought you'd figure it out. I had no idea how completely blind you could make yourself. And yes, I could have just come right out and said it. But you were just so fucking vulnerable that I could never do it. And then I hurt you anyway. But fuck, Nick—you *needed* to be hurt. You needed to have the truth kicked into you."

"It's more like a stabbing than a kicking," I tell her, just so she'll know.

"For me it's a kicking," Tris replies. "But whatever. The subject of us is through. The subject of you and Norah is not. Let me give you some free advice. She's a runner for sure—she'll run away every time without saying a word. But here's the thing—you are *not* a runner. And deep down, I don't think Norah wants to run, either. She just feels like she has to. Partly because she's a tiresome spoiled-brat smartass with no fashion sense. And partly because she's a fucking human being."

She's making sense, and that's like a rebuke, too. *Why couldn't we have had these conversations when we were together?* I think. And then I realize what I've done—I've made *when we were together* a separate, almost distant place. I still feel the hurt, but I feel much less desire to undo it.

"I'm through with you for tonight," Tris says, standing up. "Find that other fuck-up and have fucked-up children together. Don't name them after fruits or months. Be original and just name them like children."

"But she's gone," I say.

Tris snorts. "Nick, Norah's not *gone*. She's clearly *someplace*. All you have to do is find out where that is."

"Any ideas?" I ask.

"Nope," Tris answers, walking out of my life once again. "You're on your own."

I let her leave. I watch her walk into the blast of music blaring from the open door of the club.

Then I look back to the sidewalk and try to map the possibilities.

12. NORAH

I am still hungry.

I am also still tired, and still vaguely interested in my future life of sainthood, but still. I gnaw. The stale Oreo I am munching in the cab, with the cookie part soggy instead of crisp, the white center near-gelatinous—like a room temperature ice cream sandwich—is brilliant, but not coming close to quelling this hunger. I'm not sure whether the gnawing is coming from my stomach or the Arctic vicinities around that area that, earlier, eerily melted under the greenhouse effect of Nick's touch.

"Are we going or not?" the taxi driver asks me. We've sat through five rotations of the light at Houston and West Broadway while I decide where I want to go. The driver is putting up with my uncertainty because he's hopeful I won't follow through on my threat to either be driven to Jersey or file a formal complaint if he gives me any more shit about leaving the city.

"Where to, lady?"

I DON'T FUCKING KNOW!

I can only process two rational thoughts. (1) I want more stale Oreos from that Korean grocery, and (2) I don't want some stupid fucking guy to be the reason I stop liking Where's

Fluffy. I need to erase the memory of my favorite Fluffy song, their gay rights anthem "Lesbian Lap Dance," from being my last memory of the band, the song they were performing when genius girl decided to take Nick by the hand for some lap-dance action of our own. I need to get back to that fucking club.

"Back to Ludlow," I tell the driver.

Did I go too far with Nick, or not far enough? Or is it that I'm just plain unattractive? I never should have deleted all those spam e-mails advertising the vitamin supplements for fuller, firmer breasts. I'm more stacked than Caroline and Tris but mine go off in the wrong directions—over and out instead of up and in. It's probably time for me to wake up and accept the fact that I may be in need of a makeover.

The driver sighs, shakes his head, then pulls an illegal U-turn across four lanes of traffic from where we've been idling at the curb. He turns up the radio volume, perhaps hoping he will not hear me if I should change my mind again. How a former second-string player on the Kazakhstan soccer team came to be driving a graveyard-shift taxi in Manhattan and listening to Z100 instead of the standard 1010 WINS (all news, all depressing, all the time), which I had always assumed to be the one cardinal rule of taxicab radio etiquette, I don't know. Everyone has their story.

Vintage Britney sings from the pop radio station; she knows about toxic. Nick must think I'm toxic, marauding him in a closet at a Fluffy show. He didn't try to stop me when I left that room, or when I left him to get into this taxi. He didn't even wave good-bye.

The cab is careening down Bowery, whizzing by the club where earlier tonight Nick asked if I would be his girlfriend for five minutes, then made me like him, then looked right at me and made a public declaration with those magic words—"FUCK-SHIT-COCK"—that left me no choice but to make a play for him. I remember seeing Crazy Lou at the Where's Fluffy show, long after those five minutes had expired. Lou would only leave his club for someone else to close up shop if . . .

"STOP!" I shout at the driver over the music. I'm already where I'm supposed to be.

The driver slams the brakes so hard I toss my cookies—truly. The jolt sends my bag of Oreos to the floor. The taxi halted, the Kazakh poster king turns around and from the other side of the plastic divide yells back at me, "WHAT YOU WANT ANYWAY, LADY? WHAT'S THE MATTER WITH YOU?"

Tal is across the street, ushering the remaining club inhabitants from the establishment, closing up his uncle's place for the night. His post-show usual, Tal's shirt is off and he's sweeping the sidewalk. I remember Tal's chest, all lean muscle, too scrawny, too vegan. I remember my hands on Nick's chest. I liked touching Nick. He had something to grab on to. I want more touch.

I don't know what's the matter with me, driver. But if I am destined to a life of loneliness and celibacy, isn't there some side rule that entitles me to go out in one last blaze of glory? One last booty call?

Three times I start to get out of the cab to pursue that

last rite. I reach for the door handle and count the money in my wallet. Three times I stop and sit still again.

"What'll it be? Are you getting in or getting out?" the driver asks.

Over the tail end of Britney's song, I can hear The Clash wailing in my head, *Should I stay or should I go?*

I can't think with all these voices! I snap at the driver, "Lighten Up, Motherfucker." I bet Where's Fluffy are playing that conservative backlash song this very moment. Sucks that I am missing it. Nick's fault.

In a flash, the driver turns around to face me. "You want to sit in this cab and decide where to go, I don't care. It's your money." He points to the meter, still running. Time is always fucking me over. "But I'll tell you what I tell my five daughters when they get fresh. This is a gentleman you're talking to, not a casting director for *The Sopranos*. Watch your mouth or get out of the cab."

"Okay," I say. "Sorry." I bet he's a really nice dad. I bet his daughters make his favorite foods from Kazakhstan for him and nag him about getting his prostate checked regularly. "But could you at least change the station?"

"Deal," he says. The next station is playing "I Fall to Pieces" by Patsy Cline. I have no choice but to cry. The driver hands me a box of Kleenex from the front. "Want to tell me about it?"

"Boys are idiots," I tell him, sniffling. If I'm a horrid bitch from the planet Schizophrenia, it's because boys make me one. "I hope you don't let your five daughters date them."

"I try not to," he laughs. "I try."

I ask the driver to turn his headlights off while we idle at yet another curb. I want to think before I decide whether or not to talk to Tal, and I don't want Tal to notice me in this cab before I've had time to figure this out.

The last time I saw Tal was also at Lou's club, before Tal took off for the *kibbutz,* just after he dropped out of Columbia. We were in the back hallway after a show, the club room empty and darkened, smelling of beer and piss and cigarettes, littered with bottles and cups and shirts and the accumulated, spent energy of that night's mosh. Tal stood over me—too tall Tal, he's almost 6-foot-4—and had to crouch down to meet my lips. His kiss was wet, sloppy. I used to suspect this was true, but before, I didn't have much comparison. "Norah," Tal whispered, and it was the Israeli half of his inflection I heard, whereas the other tired word in his English vocabulary—"baby"—usually came out with the American side of his accent. When I was sixteen his Israeli accent saying "Norah" did sound hot to me, exciting, but at eighteen I heard it differently: it was grating, ugly, like phlegm choking up from the back of his throat instead of a wanton call.

Caroline had two guys fighting over her outside the club, and I think Tris must have been with Nick at that point, because I was all alone with Tal with nothing else to do. It was soon after our fifth and supposedly final breakup, and all I wanted from Tal was for him to shut up so we could get down to business. Tal generally preferred to read the *Forward* while whacking off in his dorm room instead of have sex with me, so it must have been a dream come true for him in the back hallway of the club—there I was, doing the work for him, without wanting anything in return. He was satisfied to let this happen and not speak to me or touch me back.

I was dead inside then, my hand cramped from the motion. Tal didn't protest when I left the hallway to step into Lou's office. He knew where I was going. He liked to be kept waiting for his release. I found the Jergens in Lou's office. I had intended to finish what I started, but stepping out of that moment, however briefly, changed my mind. I thought, I can be up on my straight-edge high horse because I don't drink or smoke or do drugs, but what does that all matter in comparison to this new low I am stooping to with Tal? He's kind of a creep; he doesn't even like me. I wondered—was it that I was frigid or that we just had no chemistry?

I placed the Jergens bottle back on the desk and snuck out the rear office door to the alley to release myself. I hadn't seen or heard from Tal since, until tonight. *She talks a great game, but when you actually get to the field, you realize it's fucking empty.* Maybe I shouldn't be so mad at Tal's review of me to Nick earlier tonight. I did last leave him with blue balls.

I am curious how Tal came to be back in my world, but getting out of this cab to ask Tal the question—*Why did you come back to Manhattan?*—may be more of a waste than the meter I am allowing to run through my time and money while I sit in this backseat. Why does anyone come here? Mere words defy that answer. The question is too big.

Whatever Tal came back here for, I'm sure he didn't come back here for me. But if he did, he's even stupider than me. How is it that two people with near-perfect SAT scores could have so little intelligence when it comes to each other?

Patsy's finished falling to pieces, and now it's Merle Haggard's turn to taunt me from the radio. The song is "Always Wanting You," a favorite of Dad's, where cynical, heartsick Merle croons about always wanting but never having his love, and about how hard it will be to face tomorrow cuz he knows he'll just be wanting her again. Doomed.

If I could have stayed in that closet with Nick, I might have figured out new degrees of wanting, tried out new moves, ones Tal never inspired in me. With me and Tal, it was straight Up/Down or In/Out. If Nick had me pinned against a wall right now, I'd be more imaginative than I ever was with Tal, stroking instead of pulling, kneading and threading, groping along with grazing, two hands instead of one, the soft scratch of fingernails included. Maybe I could inspire Nick to be a little imaginative with me, too. When Tris broke up with him, she said she knew she'd broken his heart, but she'd done him a favor, too. She'd sent him back out into the world with skills the women of his future could thank Tris for, because he certainly didn't have them when she discovered him. Fuck Tris and her Tantric knowledge.

Tomorrow is already here and I'm truly feeling Merle's bittersweet song. I shouldn't, but I do. I still want Nick.

I should have trusted him.

A gush of tears streaming down my face have replaced the light sprinkle Patsy's song inspired.

Fuck him. Fuck *me*.

Happy endings don't happen. Merle Haggard knows it, and now I know it.

Okay, I know one thing I want, something that I *can*

have. I want to conclusively end the Tal regression spiral. So maybe I lost out on Nick. But at least now I know. There are Nicks out there.

I also really want some borscht about now. "Could you please turn the lights back on?" I ask the driver. I direct him to the 24-hour Ukrainian restaurant in the East Village that's the one place Tris, Caroline, and I ever agreed on. Since we first started coming into the city on our own to hear music—as we've successively stretched parental boundaries until the restrictions and curfews have not only been lifted but banished, because we're big girls now, we might fuck up but we'll figure it all out, eventually—the three of us sometimes cap off our nights out, at least those that don't end in fights or hooking up or passing out, at the restaurant with the great borscht and the clean bathroom. I wonder if we three will ever go to this restaurant together again, or if that era is over, like mine and Tal's, and Nick and Tris's.

"Good choice," the driver tells me. He's been watching Tal's sweeping motions from the window.

I consider taking a catnap for the short drive over to the East Village but my chest is ringing. What the fuck? I forgot I was wearing Nick's—I mean my—jacket. I reach into the chest pocket to pull out a crumpled ten-dollar bill and a small, flip-up cell phone that has a photo-booth sticker of Tris stuck on it. I wouldn't have figured Nick to be the cell phone type, but then I remember, Tris gave him the phone at Christmas. When she wants to keep tabs on a boy, when she's in that mode with him, she means it. I remove the Tris photo sticker from the phone and place it on the city map beneath the taxi's back plastic divider, above the Empire State Building image, in a position so that the building appears to be giving Tris the finger.

I don't know if I should answer Nick's phone. The name flashing is "tHom."

I am a terrible person. I let two strangers take off with my sistah-girl. For all I know, Thom and Scot are the power couple of serial killers, the Ted Bundy and Aileen Wuornos of the garage-band New Jersey punk-rock scene. What if Caroline has woken up and is looking for me, like after her mom died and her dad checked out for a younger model, and Caroline would wake up in the middle of the night, scared and alone, and creep over the fence to my house? No, I shouldn't worry. My instinct may have been wrong that Nick was attracted to me, but it wasn't wrong that his friends were good guys. They'll get her home.

I answer. "Thom? Is Caroline okay?"

"Finally!" he says. "Yes, she's still asleep. Seems happy. Keeps mumbling something about cartoons and Krispy Kremes in the morning. But I've been trying to call Nick for the past hour. Didn't you guys hear the phone? Scot and I got lost coming off the parkway and then, er, we got distracted at the rest stop and the directions on my hand kinda got rubbed off. We're sitting in the parking lot of a 7-Eleven. I have no idea where we are or how to get to your house."

I try to talk Thom through it, figure out where he is, but he confuses me more, and I'm lost all over again. The taxi driver slams on his brakes again. I think we're near St. Marks Place now. "Give me that," the driver says, pointing to the phone. I like that he is law-abiding and does not try to use Nick's cell phone while the vehicle is motion.

I hand him the phone and the driver talks to Thom, figures out where he is and how to get him home to my place in Englewood Cliffs, then hands the phone back to me. "Here, Thom wants to talk to you again."

"Hi again," I say into the phone.

I hear Thom's giggle. "So how is it going? How was the date with Nick? You love him, right?"

"It's been great. We're getting married."

"Really? Can I talk to him?"

"No."

"Why not?"

"I have no idea where he is." I click off the cell.

We're at the restaurant. "You coming in?" I ask the driver. "Borscht and pierogies are on me."

He smiles at me. His daughters must have some really nice family portraits from Sears hanging in their house. "Thanks, but I'm a working man. Got to keep working. You keep the Kleenex, though."

I take the box of Kleenex out of the car and give the driver my hundred-dollar bill, the whole of my emergency cab money Dad placed in the secret crevice of my wallet. I only have enough money left in my wallet for something to eat and to take the bus back to Englewood Cliffs, so I'll have to hang out at the restaurant for a couple hours until the bus service is running again.

A crazy lady stands at the restaurant entrance, holding a Chock full o'Nuts tin can, the Wicked Witch of the Stank.

She eyeballs me, zeroing in on my chest area. Maybe she knows something about those vitamin supplements. She tells me, "Salvatore is looking for you."

I reach back into the jacket pocket for the crumpled ten-dollar bill. I donate Nick's tunnel money into the witch's can.

"No, he's not," I assure her.

13. NICK

Life fails. Songs don't always.

I'm on the curb. Taking it all in, including the nothing. Where I am, how I am, who I am, what I'm not.

It starts to come to me.

on Ludlow

the world goes so slow

all the things I don't know

closing in

on Ludlow

the sidewalk shadow

keeps pleading don't go

but you won't hear

Alright, Nick. Louder.

WHO WILL APOLOGIZE FOR HOW

WE ARE?

WHO WILL NAVIGATE WHEN WE'VE

GONE THIS FAR?

ANSWER ME

ANSWER THIS

ANSWER ALL THE QUESTIONS THAT

I'M TOO AFRAID TO ASK

ON LUDLOW

YOU LET ME KNOW

AND I LET YOU GO

AND WE WERE WRONG WRONG

WRONG

ON LUDLOW

THERE'S A SHADOW

THAT LETS THE TRUTH SHOW

AND WE WERE WRONG WRONG

WRONG

NEVER AGAIN

IS WHAT I ALWAYS SAY

NEVER AGAIN

IS WHAT I ALWAYS SAY

NEVER AGAIN

IS WHAT I AL WAYS SAY

Take it back down.

on Ludlow

it's just a stone's throw

from where we could go

to where we are

on Ludlow

find me on Ludlow

on Ludlow

find me here . . .

"Dude! That's pretty kickass!"

Dev slaps me on the back and sits next to me, his hair a ball of dance-induced sweat, the moisture making his shirt fit even tighter than when it began the night.

"You're not in there for Where's Fluffy?"

"Nah. Needed to take a break. You think it's easy being the cutest damn underage lead singer on the queercore scene? I can't work it all the time, man."

"Where's Randy?"

"Who?"

"Randy."

"Huh?"

"From Are You Randy? You were, uh, with him before?"

"Oh! You mean Ted! He'll be out in a few. Wanted to dance off the last song. Isn't he high voltage?"

Dev's got his mischievous, smitten gleam in his eye, so I nod in agreement. Sometimes Dev only has the mischievousness, and none of the smittenosity—that's when I usually worry about the other guy's heart. But when Dev gets bitten by the swoony bug, I know it isn't just sex that he's after.

"So where's Tris?" he asks now.

"Inside. Why?"

"I dunno. I figured you two would be together."

"Dev . . . Tris and I broke up like four weeks ago."

"Fuck! I totally forgot. Sorry, man."

"No problem."

Dev looks at me for a moment, then smacks his forehead.

"Wait! There's another girl tonight, isn't there? I saw you, like, groping."

"You could say that."

"I just did!"

"What?"

"Say that. I could, and I did."

This, for Dev, is what usually passes as genius.

Now he puts his arm around me, snuggles in. He loves to do this, and I never really mind. It's not sexual so much as comforting.

"My poor straight-edge straightboy," he says. "Nobody should be alone on a night like this."

"But I have you, Dev," I reply, trying to lighten things up.

"Ain't that the truth. At least until Ted comes back."

"I know."

"You know what it's all about, Nick?"

"What what's all about?"

"It, Nick. What *it's* all about."

"No."

"The Beatles."

"What about The Beatles?"

"They nailed it."

"Nailed what?"

"Everything."

"What do you mean?"

Dev takes his arm and puts it right against mine, skin to skin, sweat on sweat, touch on touch. Then he glides his hand into mine and intertwines our fingers.

"This," he says. "This is why The Beatles got it."

"I'm afraid I'm not following . . ."

"Other bands, it's about sex. Or pain. Or some fantasy. But The Beatles, they knew what they were doing. You know the reason The Beatles made it so big?"

"What?"

" 'I Wanna Hold Your Hand.' First single. Fucking brilliant. Perhaps the most fucking brilliant song ever written. Because they nailed it. That's what everyone wants. Not 24-7 hot wet sex. Not a marriage that lasts a hundred years. Not a Porsche or a blow job or a million-dollar crib. No. They wanna hold your hand. They have such a feeling that *they can't hide*. Every single successful love song of the past fifty years can be traced back to 'I Wanna Hold Your Hand.' And every single successful love story has those unbearable and unbearably exciting moments of hand-holding. Trust me. I've thought a lot about this."

" 'I Wanna Hold Your Hand,' " I repeat.

"And so you are, my friend. So you are."

He closes his eyes now, fingers still folded into mine. Even Dev's breathing is rock 'n' roll, full of kicks and sputters. I angle my head on top of his. We sit there for a second, watching traffic.

"I think I blew it," I say.

"With Tris?"

"No. With Norah. With Tris, I didn't have a chance. But tonight, with Norah—it might've been a chance."

"So?"

"So what?"

"So what are you going to do about it?"

"I don't know—sulk?"

Dev removes his hand from mine and squeezes me lightly on the shoulder.

"You're damn pretty when you sulk," he tells me, "but in this case, I think a more active course might be advantageous."

"Where the hell are you getting these long words from?" I have to ask.

"You, stupid. 'If you act courageous / it could be advantageous / to make me act outrageous / all over your blank pages'—did you think I was, like, learning these songs phonetically?"

" 'My love ain't hypothetical / or pronounced for you phonetical / so it might just be heretical / if you don't love me back,'" I quote in return.

Dev nods. "Exactly."

"Where do we come up with this shit?" I ask. "I mean, where do these words all come from? I sit here on this sidewalk and they just *appear* to me."

"Maybe they're always there and you just need to live enough life to get them to make sense," Dev says.

Someone whistles a birdcall behind us. Dev and I both turn, and there's Ted just out of the club, shining like a diamond under a spotlight. He's keeping a respectful distance, but I can tell he's waiting.

"You gonna go hold his hand?" I ask Dev playfully.

"Hell, yes," Dev says, sitting up now. "Don't get me wrong—we're totally going to make the beast with two backs tonight. But if we do it right, it's going to feel like holding hands."

There's no way Ted could've heard us. But when Dev walks over to him, Ted offers his palm. I watch them walk down the street, hand in hand. I don't think they notice, but their legs are in perfect rhythm. Before they round the corner, they both turn as one and wave a goodnight to me.

I'm on my own again. I decide to check my messages . . . and realize that not only have I lost my fucking jacket, but I've also lost my fucking phone. So many indignities and I start to feel indignant. But that's *nothing* compared to trying to find a pay phone on Ludlow Street at three or so in the morning. I walk all the way back to Houston before I find one on the corner of a deli. The receiver feels like it's covered with pond scum, and the dial tone seems to be coming from North Dakota. The first three quarters are returned to the drop slot. I am about to lose my shit entirely, but then the next two quarters stay put and the volume button amps things up enough that I can actually hear the call start.

Norah answers on the fourth ring.

"Who the hell is this?" she asks.

I mean, I knew she would answer. But still I'm dumbstruck.

"Is Nick there?" I finally ask.

"No," she says. "He's out defeating a minor threat. Do you want to call back for his voice mail?"

It's like I can't help it. I am absolutely falling back into conversation with her.

"Can you give him a message?" I ask.

"Do I need a pen? Cuz if I do, you're so fucking out of luck."

"No. Could you just tell him that he totally blew it when he let Norah get away in that cab?"

There's a pause. "Who the fuck is this?"

"And could you let him know that I'm really fucking relieved that he has finally unshackled himself from that Tris bitch?"

"You're kidding, right?"

"And could you pass on the message that it's not enough to be sitting alone on a sidewalk writing a song for a girl if you don't have the guts to at least try talking to her again?"

Another pause. "Are you serious?"

"Where are you?"

"Veselka. Where are you?"

"Doesn't matter," I say. "I'll be at Veselka soon. In the meantime, can you pass on my message?"

I hang up before she can reply.

14. NORAH

That is so rude, hanging up on a person like that.

I refuse to believe that call just happened. I'm so sleepy I'm hallucinating.

Just in case, I go into the bathroom, splash some cold water on my face to wake the fuck up, finger through my hair to make it look tousled in an attractive way but not so attractive that it looks like I tousled it because I care what it looks like, and reach down inside my shirt to rearrange my boobs. Salvatore looks the other way.

When I get back to the table, it's heaped with food: the bowl of hot borscht (better than my bubbe's, but I'll never admit that to her face), half a dozen pierogies, some kielbasa. The blintzes should be following soon. What can I say, I am very, very hungry, and I am craving meat *bad*. I can save the leftovers for the witch lady or some other street person outside.

I dive into the food like I have just been released from prison. I think I have borscht dribbling down my chin when I manage to look up from my quantum inhalation. He's here. Holy shit. Memo to Merle Haggard: Miracles really do happen.

I am still embarrassed, but I also remember, I am renewed,

destined for my certain future as a U.N. humanitarian. I am immune from throwing myself at him again, seeing as how I've committed to a future life of loneliness and celibacy. It probably won't be so bad. I will never get an STD, I will never have to worry about a condom breaking again, and the lack of sex, or even having to think about it, want it, strive for it, will probably lead me to a higher plane of enlightenment, like the Dalai Lama. So it's all good. Zero balance. Nick can relax. I won't gobble him, too.

Nick doesn't speak at first, he just sits down and butters a piece of challah toast and lays right into that, equaling my fervor. Between swallows, he asks, "How many fucking people did you order food for anyway?" He takes a sip of my Coke, belches, then repeats my last words to him back to me. " 'You are absolved'? What the fuck did that mean?" He sounds hostile but he's got that fucking half smile laced back on his lips.

I am determined to sulk, but the truth is, I want to lick him all over. I cannot believe he is here. I want to do truly nasty things to him. With him.

I try to sound blasé. "It means, we met under kind of strange circumstances and spent a few kind of strange hours together, but just because I made an asshole of myself doesn't mean you have to go all Nice Guy and like try to push our whatever-it-was any farther. Anyway, we don't even know each other and we've never even been properly introduced—"

Nick interrupts me by extending his hand, slick with traces of butter. "I'm Nick," he says. "I'm from a swingin' little hood called Hoboken. Where's Fluffy were my favorite band until tonight. I write songs. I was dumped by a wildebeest but I'm working on getting over it. And you?"

I shake his hand and try hard to suppress a smile. I don't owe him that. "I'm Norah," I say. "From Englewood fuckin' not-swingin' Cliffs. Where's Fluffy were also my favorite band until tonight. I love songs that are written. I dumped a wildebeest and he dumped me and it's been this endless miserable spiral, but I'm also getting over it."

"Hi, Norah," he says.

"Hi, Nick," I answer.

"Can I have my fucking jacket back?"

"No." I deserve some reward for my rejection and for my future life of celibacy and good deeds.

"Why?"

"Because Salvatore wants me to have it."

"He told you that?"

"He did."

"But what if the jacket didn't really belong to Salvatore? What if it wasn't his to give you? What if it really belonged to his evil twin, Salamander, who only had Salvatore's name stenciled on so people would mistake him for the good twin and then Salamander would be free to carry on with his nefarious mission in life?"

"What nefarious mission would that be?"

"You know, world domination, that whole thing."

"World domination is exhausting and cliché. People ought to just focus on being individual responsible citizens of the earth instead of assholes. And you can tell that to Salamander next time he comes asking you for his jacket. Tell him me and Salvatore are starting our own new world order. It's called the Chill the Fuck Out and Let the Girl Have the Jacket movement."

"Will there be T-shirts and pins for this new movement?"

"Probably. We're looking into luggage insignia as well, maybe even some corporate product endorsements from Nike or IBM."

I don't realize I am laughing, or even moving, until Nick takes a strand of hair that's fallen in front of my face and tucks it behind my ear and for a second I feel my breath on his arm. Because now we are looking at each other eye to eye and there's possibly forgiveness in there, and it's possibly mutual, and for that second my stomach feels this momentary lurch of hope, it's the same feeling as dread, and because I am a fucking loser who never learns, I blurt out, "I sort of know you already, actually."

"Huh?" he says.

The food rush has infiltrated my brain, made it hazy, unable to distinguish between flirting and saying too much. "I feel like I have kind of known you, through Tris. She and I aren't friends exactly, only we're not not-friends exactly, either. You made some amazing mixes for that bitch, wrote some great lyrics. I would see that stuff you gave her and always think, Hey, I wouldn't mind knowing this guy. Not like I wanted to go after Tris's boyfriend or anything, and I'm not a stalker, at least I don't think I am, but I guess . . ." Oh, fuck it, why not just be honest? He's not the one absolved—*I* am. ". . . I guess I just thought you might be a cool person even before I'd met you, based on purely circumstantial evidence. So you don't think I randomly throw myself at just any guy."

There is a silence, and in that silence I hate all boys, for never knowing the right thing to say. "Why did you leave?" he asks. *Why did YOU stop?*

"National security emergency. Salvatore and I got beeped. Turned out to be a false alarm." Why do you *think* I left, beautiful moron?

And we're at a stalemate. We eat.

"Where are your friends?" I finally say after a couple pierogies. Just to say something. Again. I'm sure his boys will be rolling through any moment to retrieve him, probably steal my blintzes. Nick must have found me only so he could get his fucking phone back.

Nick says, "Dev left with Ted."

"Ted?"

"You know, Ted from Are You Randy?"

"There's no Ted from Are You Randy? There's Randy and a bunch of other guys, none named Ted."

"Then who's Randy?" Nick asks.

"The guy who was trying to get with Caroline!"

"Who's Caroline?"

"For fuck's sake, who's TED?"

"The guy Dev hooked up with!"

"That's HUNTER. From Hunter Does Hunter."

"Oh," Nick says. "I get it now." He draws a map on the paper placemat on the table. "Dev's with Ted, who's also Hunter, but he's not Randy, who wanted Caroline, who I guess is the girl in the back of the van with Thom and Scot?"

I place my hand over his fist. "YES!"

It's almost like I've shared another dance with Johnny Castle, and I must be sleeping because this is not real, Nick is not real, this is not happening. I hope I don't wake up too soon. I pinch his thigh to check, and he leans over to me, and we're both smiling in anticipation and our eyes are meeting and something I think very natural and sweet is about to happen here, except . . .

A Beast stands over our table. It points at me. "I need to talk to you. Come into my office." Tris whips around and heads toward the bathroom. I'm amazed that even with her thick black roots peeking through her platinum-blond hair, the eyeliner and lipstick on her face smudged from the night's adventures, her eyes bloodshot from fatigue, she still manages to look hot. It's so wrong.

I stand up from the table and wiggle my index finger at Nick. He'll never get it, but I borrow from *Heathers* as I leave him to follow Tris. " 'A true friend's work is never done,' " I singsong.

" 'Bulimia is so '87, Heather,' " he answers.

HOLY SHIT squared. I think I just had my first orgasm.

Tris is peeing when I walk in. She is not a person who cares about privacy. But I close the door behind me anyway and say, "What the fuck are you doing here?" She gives me this great castoff, like a gift fallen from the sky, and yet she seems determined that I should not open it or enjoy it.

"I lost my date and I knew I would find you here, borscht bitch. I need cab money home. I figure you owe me. Fifty bucks ought to cover a gypsy cab back to Jersey and a Starbucks run." She wipes, stands up, flushes. "So can I have it?" She shoves me aside to wash her hands at the sink.

"How do you figure I owe you?"

"You know, I'm giving you Nick."

"Are you really?" I ask. Because we should get this clear once and for all.

"I really am," she says, applying a fresh coat of lipstick. I believe her.

"I think I really like him," I say.

"He likes you, too. Just don't name your children after months or fruits. Promise me."

"What?" I say.

She faces me. "Are you going to give me the fifty bucks or not?"

"Don't you think Nick is worth more than that?"

"Bitch, I'm not trying to quantify the value of a human being. I just need to get home. And don't cry poor because I know you have a secret stash of emergency money tucked in some pocket." She leans over me and, honest to Allah, frisks me. "Jesus, you're stacked! Why do you hide it under these huge shirts all the time?"

I thought I used up my emergency money when I gave my secret stash to the cabdriver who got me here, but then I remember the fifty-dollar bill Thom gave me earlier to take Nick out on a date intended to free the boy of Tris's ghost. So much for that fund. Thom and Scot couldn't have anticipated that the wildebeest herself would profit from their contribution to Nick's night out.

I shove Tris away and reach inside the inner pocket of my flannel shirt. I hand Tris the fifty-spot. "Thank you!" she snaps. She turns to leave, but I pull her back.

"Tris?"

"What, bitch?"

"Am I really frigid?"

She sighs. "Of course you're not frigid. Don't believe all the propaganda Caroline and Tal have laid on you. I saw you kissing Nick earlier tonight. Looked to me like you two knew what you were doing."

"But I don't," I say.

"Don't what?"

"Know what I'm doing."

Tris rolls her eyes. She walks over and points her index finger at me. "I'm gonna give you a little help here, but first you have to swear to me you didn't know Nick before tonight and this wasn't some . . . whadyacallit . . . streetlamp setup to trick me—"

"Streetlamp trick?"

"You know, to make me think I'm going crazy when really you've been plotting this all along."

"That's *Gaslight,* Tris. Not streetlamp. Remember that movie my mother made us watch at my eleventh birthday slumber party? And no, I never met Nick before tonight." I raise my hand and make the Girl Scout honor pledge sign.

"Okay, then," Tris says. "I believe you."

She takes her gum from her mouth and presses it against the wall behind me, pinning me there with her upraised arms. Then she presses against me and my eyes are still open and they see her coming in and HOLY SHIT triple squared, she says, "Kiss your partner's upper lip." She kisses my upper lip, softly, gently. "That's yang." Her lips move down. "Kiss your partner's bottom lip." She kisses my bottom lip, more urgently. "That's yin." She pulls away but her left hand is now under the back of my shirt, pressed against the small of my spine. "Start by opening up your chakras, like that."

I don't say anything. My lips remain parted, not sure if the lesson is over.

"Or," Tris says, "you can try this one." With both hands, she pulls my face to hers. She sucks my upper lip between her lips, and then her tongue is in my mouth, caressing the middle area between my upper lip and my gums. I never even noticed that area was there. Yeah, I'm pretty sure I'm not frigid. "That's the frenulum," she says when she's done. She pats down her hair. "That little connective tissue inside your mouth. It's a Hot Spot. You can use that one on Nick, you have my permission. I don't think I ever used that one on him so it's not like you'd be copying me."

I'm standing against the wall, unsure of what to say or do. Now I'm sure I'm in a dream.

Tris says, "Or you can be inventive. Go on. Try me."

What the hell? I turn my head at an angle and lean in to her face. I place my hands on her hips, press against her. Slowly, I kiss her upper lip, yang, suck on her lower lip, yin, but instead of following up with tongue, which her mouth definitely seems to want, I return to her upper lip and give it some gentle bites.

She pulls back. "Nip kissing! Good instinct, Norah. See?

You're not frigid. Gotta be careful with that one, though. Only do it with a partner you trust. Those teeth can get dangerous with the wrong person."

"How do you know so much?" I ask her. I mean, I know she's a groupie bitch, but she's barely voting age—she hasn't had *that* much time to acquire so much knowledge.

"Hello, bitch, I can Google sexual techniques just as well as you could if you wanted. It's not brain science here." She turns to leave and reaches for the door handle, then pauses and turns back around to face me. "But, Norah?"

"Yes?" I whisper.

"Get to know him first. You and he are not the one-night-stand types. You're all sensitive and shit. Don't go too fast."

And she's gone.

"Bye, Tris!" I gasp.

From the open door, I see her breeze past Nick on her way out of the restaurant. She tells him, "I told you that you'd find her *someplace*! Good job! And good luck with that one. You're gonna need it. I almost feel sorry for you."

I feel less sorry for Nick now. Maybe he's not some poor schmuck. I totally get how he got so whipped.

15. NICK

While they're in the bathroom together, I try to distract myself by coming up with a list of things that could be worse than having your vehement ex drag your current she's-so-frickin'-cool girl away for some cubicle camaraderie (or conflict). I come up with the following:

- Having your pubic hair trimmed with garden shears.
- Having your pubic hair trimmed with garden shears by a frat guy who's had twelve shots of Jägermeister.
- Having your pubic hair trimmed with garden shears by a frat guy who's had twelve shots of Jägermeister during an 8.6 earthquake.
- Having your pubic hair trimmed with garden shears by a frat guy who's had twelve shots of Jägermeister during an 8.6 earthquake *with lite jazz playing.*

I have to stop there. It's just too horrifying.

It's amazing how little I trust Tris, considering that I like to pay lip service to the fact that trust is an essential ingredient to love.

Best case scenario:

She's saying, "Really, he was just too good for me, and I

always felt like he could do better . . . like with a girl like you. And, man, is he hot in bed."

Worst case scenario:

She's saying, "There was this one time, we were flipping through the channels, and he stopped on *Pocahontas,* and the next thing I knew, he had *a total hard-on.*" (She will not mention where her hands were at the time.) "And, man, he is one lousy fuck, in more ways than one."

Deep breaths. I am taking deep breaths.

Composure. Which, for me, means composing.

Why the fuck does my fate get decided

in the ladies' room?

Sitting tongue-tied as I get derided

in the ladies' room.

Employees must wash their hands of me

in the ladies' room

Lock the door and throw away the plea

in the ladies' room.

Maybe this is my way of creating the illusion of control over something I have no control over. Like, if it's just a story I'm telling or a song I'm singing, then I'll be okay because I'm the guy who's providing the words. Which is not the way life works at all. Or at least not when it's unfair.

I guess the cool thing is that I really wasn't happy to see Tris. For the first time in what seems like ever. She walked in the door and my heart sank to hell.

It was strange enough to think that Norah knew who I was before I knew who she was. That she'd been in Tris's orbit without me noticing. But I guess you don't see the planets when you're staring at the sun. You just get blinded.

The fact that she knew me makes this more real. I made my first impression without knowing I was making an impression at all. She knows at least a little of who I am, and she's here anyway. Hopefully for longer than the next two minutes.

The waitress probably thinks I'm the worst kind of perv, because I can't stop staring at the bathroom door.

Finally it opens, and Tris comes out alone. And my first thought, honest to Godspeed You Black Emperor!, is *What the fuck have you done to Norah? Where is she?*

But Tris isn't staying long enough to be asked any questions. She just pushes past the table, yelling to me, "I told you that you'd find her *someplace*! Good job! And good luck with that one. You're gonna need it. I almost feel sorry for you."

And all I can think to say is:

"thanks."

But I don't say anything more. I let her leave. I mean, I don't want her to stay. And yes, that makes this the first time

I'm off of her without still getting off on the thought of her. I believe some cultures call this progress.

Norah's looking really flustered as she comes back to the table, her face flushed, her pulse clearly up a notch or two. It must've been one hell of a confrontation.

"Are you okay?" I ask.

She nods absently. Then she looks at me again and it's like our conversation kicks back in. She's with me again.

"Yeah," she says. "She just needed some money."

"And you gave her what she wanted?"

"I guess we have a lot in common, don't we?"

"She's a fucking force of nature," I say.

"She certainly is."

"But to hell with her."

Norah seems a little startled.

"What?" she says.

"I don't know what she said to you, and I probably don't want to know. Just like I don't want to know why you ordered all this meat, or where you got your flannel—not that there's anything wrong with it. That's not what I want to know."

She defiantly spears a piece of kielbasa and, before putting it in her mouth, asks, "So what do you want to know?"

What the hell are we doing here?

Is this incredibly foolish?

Am I even ready to have this conversation?

"What I want to know," I say, "is which song you liked the most on the mixes I made Tris."

She chews for a second. Swallows. Drinks some water.

"That's what you want to know?"

"It seems like a place to start."

"Honestly?"

"Yeah."

She doesn't even have to think. She just says, "The noticing song. I don't know its name."

Whoa. I mean, I thought she would name something from Patti Smith or Fugazi or Jeff Buckley or Where's Fluffy. Or even one of the Bee Gees songs I put on, to be funny. I didn't think she'd choose something I wrote and sang. It wasn't even supposed to be on that mix. But one night I was just so wired from being with Tris that I had to stay up until I turned the evening into a song. I recorded it onto my computer, than stuck it on as a hidden track for the mix I gave her the next day.

Tris never mentioned it to me.

Not once.

" 'March Eighteenth,' " I say.

"What?"

"That's the name of the song. I mean, it doesn't really have a name. I can't believe you remember it."

"I loved it."

"Really?" I have to ask.

"Really," she says. And from the tone of her voice, I can tell it's a real "really." Then, to my amazement, she leans in and starts to sing the refrain. Not in a full voice, so everyone in the restaurant can hear. But like a stereo turned low, or a car radio on a lonely night. She sings me back to me:

The way you're singing in your sleep

The way you look before you leap

The strange illusions that you keep

You don't know

But I'm noticing

The way your touch turns into arcs

The way you slide into the dark

The beating of my open heart

You don't know

But I'm noticing

And I'm moved, it's so beautiful. Not what I wrote, but to have it given back like this. To have her remember the words and the tune. To hear it in her voice.

She is blushing furiously, so I don't clap or do anything like that. Instead I shake my head and hope my amazement is translating.

"Wow," I say.

"Yeah, that's what I thought. Although, in all honesty, the first time I heard it, it caught me on a really bad day."

"I can't believe you—"

"I promise I'm not a stalker or anything. I promise I've forgotten all the other songs."

"Really?"

"Can we change the subject?"

And I find myself saying, "It wasn't really about her." And finding it's true.

"What do you mean?" Norah asks.

"It was about the feeling, you know? She caused it in me, but it wasn't about her. It was about my reaction, what I wanted to feel and then convinced myself that I felt, because I wanted it that bad. That illusion. It was love because I created it as love."

Norah nods. "With Tal, it was the way he always said goodnight. Isn't that stupid? At first on the phone, and then when he'd drop me off, and even later when we were together and drifting off to sleep. He always wished me a goodnight and made it sound like it really was a wish. It's probably just something his mother always did when he was a kid. A habit. But I thought, *This is caring. This is real*. It could erase so many other things. That simple goodnight."

"I don't think Tris ever wished me a goodnight."

"Well, Tal sure as hell didn't inspire me to write songs."

"That's too bad," I say. "Tal rhymes with fucking *everything*."

Norah thinks for a second. "You never put her name in any of the songs, did you?"

I go through the entire playlist, then shake my head.

"Why not?"

"I guess it didn't occur to me."

Norah's phone rings and she pulls it out of her pocket.

She looks at the screen and mumbles, "Caroline." I see she's about to answer it, and find myself saying, "Don't."

"Don't?"

"Yeah."

Another ring.

"What if it's an emergency?"

"She'll call back. Look, I want us to take a walk."

"A walk?"

Ring number three.

"Yeah. You, me, and the city. I want to talk to you."

"Are you serious?"

"Not as a rule, but in this case yes."

Ring.

"Where will we go?"

"Wherever. It's only"—I look at my watch—"four in the morning."

Pause.

Silence.

Voice mail.

Norah bites her bottom lip.

"Thinking about it?" I ask uneasily.

"No. Just thinking about where to go. Somewhere nobody will find us."

"Like Park Avenue?"

And Norah tilts her head, looks at me a little askew, and says, "Yes, like Park Avenue."

And then she utters a word I never in a zillion years thought I'd ever hear her utter:

"Midtown."

It's ridiculous, but we take the subway. Even more ridiculous, it's the 6 train that we take, the most notoriously slow local in all of Manhattan. At four in the morning, we're on the platform for a good twenty minutes—the time it would've taken us to walk—but I don't mind the delay because we're talking all over the place, hitting *Heathers* and peanut butter preferences and favorite pairs of underwear and Tris's occasional body odor and Tal's body hair fetish and the fate of the Olsen twins and the number of times we've seen rats in the subway and our favorite graffiti ever—all in what seems like a single sentence that lasts the whole twenty minutes. Then we're in the weird fluorescence of the subway car, sliding into each other when the train stops and starts, making comments with our eyes about the misbegotten drunkards, business-suit stockbroker frat boys, and weary night travelers that share our space. I am having a fucking great time, and the amazing thing is that I realize it even as it's happening. I think Norah's getting into it, too. Sometimes when we slide together, we take a few seconds to separate ourselves. We're not to the point of deliberately touching again, but we're not about to turn down a good accident.

We get out of the subway at Grand Central and walk north on Park. It's completely empty, the skyscrapers standing guard up and down the avenue, sleeping sentries of the important world.

"It feels like we're in a canyon," Norah says.

"What freaks me out is how many of the buildings still have lights on. I mean, there have to be thousands of lights in each building that are left on for the night. That can't be very efficient."

"There are probably still people working. Checking their e-mail. Making another million. Screwing someone over while they sleep."

"Or maybe," I say, "they just think it's pretty."

Norah snorts. "You're right. That must be it."

"Does your dad work around here?"

"No. He's all about downtown. Yours?"

Now it's my turn to snort. "Not employed at the present," I say. "Definitely for lack of trying."

"I'm sorry."

"No worries."

"Are your parents still together?"

"In the sense that they live in the same house, yeah. Yours?"

"They were high school sweethearts. Married twenty-five years now. Still happy and still doing it. Complete freaks of nature."

We sit down on the edge of one of the corporate fountains, watching the headlight show of passing traffic.

"So, do you come here often?" I joke.

"Yeah. I know, I'm so bridge-and-tunnel—for as long as I've been able to catch the train, I've been sneaking into the city to go to Midtown. Hang out with the bankers, merge some mergers and acquire some acquisitions. The whole thing just reeked of sex and rock 'n' roll to me. Can't you feel it in the air? Close your eyes. Feel it?"

I do close my eyes. I hear the cars passing, not just in

front of us, but on streets throughout the grid. I hear the buildings yawning into space. I hear my heartbeat. I have this momentary fantasy that she's going to lean over and kiss me again. But enough time goes by for me to know this isn't going to happen. When I open them, I find her looking at me.

"You're cute. You know that?" she says.

I have no idea what to say to that. So it just hangs in the air, until I finally say, "You're just saying that to get me to take off my clothes and frolic in the fountain."

"Am I really that transparent? Fuck!" Her look is quizzical, but I don't feel like this is a quiz.

"We could go break into St. Patrick's instead," I suggest.

"With our clothes off?"

"I'd have to keep on my socks. Do you know what kind of people touch the ground there?"

"I'll have to say ix-nay on the athedral-cay. I can see the headlines now: 'RECORD EXEC DAUGHTER FOUND PLAYING PORNISH PRANKS IN PATRICK'S. *"We thought she was such a nice Jewish girl," neighbors say.*' "

"You're Jewish?" I ask.

Norah looks at me like I just asked if she was really a girl.

"*Of course* I'm Jewish."

"So what's that like?" I ask.

"Are you kidding me?"

Do I look like I'm kidding her?

"No," I say. "Really. What's that like?"

"I don't know. It's just something that *is*. It's not something that's *like*."

"Well, what are your favorite things about it?"

"Like the fact that there are eight days of Hanukkah?"

"Sure, if that means something to you."

"All it really means to me is that I was slightly less bitter about not having a tree when I was a kid."

"So what about the real things?" I ask. I want to know more.

"The real things?"

"Yeah. Try."

She thinks for a second. "Okay. There's one part of Judaism I really like. Conceptually, I mean. It's called *tikkun olam*."

"Tikkun olam," I repeat.

"Exactly. Basically, it says that the world has been broken into pieces. All this chaos, all this discord. And our job—everyone's job—is to try to put the pieces back together. To make things whole again."

"And you believe that?" I ask. Not as a challenge. As a genuine question.

She shrugs, then negates the shrug with the thought in her eyes. "I guess I do. I mean, I don't know how the world broke. And I don't know if there's a God who can help us fix it. But the fact that the world is broken—I absolutely believe that. Just look around us. Every minute—every single second—there are a million things you could be thinking about. A million things you could be *worrying* about. Our world—don't you just feel we're becoming more and more fragmented? I used to think that when I got older, the world would make so much more sense. But you know what? The older I get, the more confusing it is to me. The more complicated it is.

Harder. You'd think we'd be getting better at it. But there's just more and more chaos. The pieces—they're everywhere. And nobody knows what to do about it. I find myself grasping, Nick. You know that feeling? That feeling when you just want the right thing to fall into the right place, not only because it's right, but because it will mean that such a thing is still possible? I want to believe in that."

"Do you really think it's getting worse?" I ask. "I mean, aren't we better off than we were twenty years ago? Or a hundred?"

"We're better off. But I don't know if the world's better off. I don't know if the two are the same thing."

"You're right," I say.

"Excuse me?"

"I said, 'You're right.'"

"But nobody ever says, 'You're right.' Just like that."

"Really?"

"Really."

She leans into me a little then. Not accidental. But still somehow it feels like an accident—us being here, this night. As if she's reading my mind, she says, "I appreciate it." Then her head falls to my shoulder, and all I can feel is her fitting there. I look up, trying to find the sky behind the building, trying to find at least a trace of the stars. When I can't, I close my eyes and try to conjure my own, glad that Norah's not reading my mind just now, because I don't know how I'd react if anyone knew me like that. As we sit in that city silence, which is not so much silence as light noise, my mind drifts back a few minutes, thinking about what she said.

Then it hits me.

"Maybe we're the pieces," I say.

Norah's head doesn't move from my arm. "What?" she asks. I can tell from her voice that her eyes are still closed.

"Maybe that's it," I say gently. "With what you were talking about before. The world being broken. Maybe it isn't that we're supposed to find the pieces and put them back together. Maybe *we're* the pieces."

She doesn't reply, but I can tell she's listening carefully. I feel like I'm understanding something for the first time, even if I'm not entirely sure what it is yet.

"Maybe," I say, "what we're supposed to do is come together. That's how we stop the breaking."

Tikkun olam.

16. NORAH

Nick and I have fallen silent again but I don't think it's the uncomfortable variety of silence. I think it's dawn closing in and we're both as sleepy as we are stimulated, and as Saturday rolls into Sunday, it's almost mesmerizing to look up the canyon to the clouds, murky gray and yellow from the city lights, while on the ground the banking and secretarial types smoke outside the building lobbies as Lincoln Town Cars idle at the curb, waiting to take the overnight workers home. The scions of the financial world here do not appear to notice or care that time could stop at any moment, so why not obey that 'on the seventh day ye shall rest' thing? At least, go out and enjoy your life. Like I am now, watching you.

But I am so greedy to learn more about Nick that I can't bear the silence, even if it's a nice one. Maybe the way to find out more about him is to tell him more about me. So I inform him, "I get my flannel in the men's department at Marshalls."

"My mom loves that store," he says.

"Your mom is smart."

I wait. Will he tell me more about his mom?

While my mind plays through the information I've compiled about him so far on this night, my mouth is talking stupid fucking Marshalls because my head is still getting around Nick's words about *tikkun olam: Maybe it isn't that we're supposed to find the pieces and put them back together. Maybe we're the pieces.*

Because I am trying to put together the pieces that make up this guy. Let's review. Straight-edge guy who survived a six-month relationship with Tris. Bassist in a queercore band, promising lyricist. Can get profound (at least for a *goyim*) in the matters of *tikkun olam*. And he's a fucking great kisser—but one who said NO to the no-strings-attached sex that was basically offered to him by an idiot girl in a closet at a Where's Fluffy show a couple hours ago, and yet somehow he still managed to pop up at Veselka for her later (pretty fucking sexy move); but then he didn't make a move on her on the 6 train when opportunity and ambience were just so converging as the lights dimmed and the train lurched their bodies together. What am I supposed to do with this guy?

As I lean my head on Nick's arm, I can smell him up close and personal without the club haze of beer and smoke, and he smells faintly of either a cologne spritz or like he had an aromatherapy massage at some spa before this night started, which strikes me as a disturbingly high-maintenance scent for a punk boy. His scent sends the pieces in my mind together, into finally making sense of him.

I may have to issue a retraction to Randy from Are You Randy?

There's no fucking way this Nick guy is one hundred percent straight.

As if to prove my suspicion, Nick takes some Chapstick

from his jeans pocket and rubs it on his lips. I'm a Blistex whore myself, so it's not the Chapstick that alerts me; it's the cherry flavor.

If he turns out to be gay, I will be furious. They get all the good ones! I will have no choice but to take it personally. The loss of Nick to the other team would be a huge blow, like, up there with the losses of Scottie "not-at-all" Gross, in whom I invested five solid years of preteen Sunday school crushing and who would have been my first kiss the night of my bat mitzvah if stupid fucking Ethan Weiner hadn't gotten to Scottie first, and also babelicious George Michael, my ultimate tragedy-to-redemption *Behind the Music* icon, who in a just and good world would have been my older man–Lolita secret fling experience. SO NOT FAIR!

Then again. Maybe the simple diagnosis of either *hetero* or *homo* is misleading. Maybe there's just *sexuality,* and it's bendable and unpredictable, like a circus performer, which I used to want to be, and hey, that could be a good option worth pursuing now that I fucked up my college admissions and the *kibbutz* thing sure ain't gonna happen. I'd like to be bendy like a circus performer. Maybe Tris would come see my show sometime and I could find out more about her groupie bitch skills.

Wherever Nick's sexuality lies (lays?—whatever, same diff), the bottom line is: This Nick guy is too good to be true. He writes amazing songs. He is so fucking cute. He's damn smart. And damn sensitive. He's given me more adventure and confusion in one night than I've had in a lifetime. My heart is aching again, scared, because I want to know EVERYTHING about him now. The more he gives me, the more I want. I want to know about his plans for the future, about his family, about his music, his dreams, his sorrows, all that sentimental bullshit.

I wonder if he shares my feeling that the Fluffy track "Hideous Becomes You" is just the most beautiful love song ever, and would he ever sing that one to me sometime? Because I already sang his noticing song back to him, and I told him about *tikkun olam,* which seems like such a random thing but it's really important and sacred to me, and I'm thinking if we name our first son Salvatore, that's not the name of a fruit or a month, and lots of not 100% straight people procreate, right?

What's of more concern: If I don't shut down my brain soon, my imagination will take off so far about what *could* be with this guy, that nothing will ever be able to just *be.*

Nick is right, the Olsen twins do have a worrisome co-dependent relationship. I understand those bitches, though, I really do. Much as I want to learn more about Nick, I also want to take a time-out so I can tell Caroline about him. If Caroline were here, we could dissect Nick via *My So-Called Life* script/ Jordan Catalano moments.

Rayanne: I think part of him is partly interested in you. Definitely. I mean, he's got other things on his mind.

Angela: But that's the part that's so unfair. I have nothing else on my mind. How come I have to be the one sitting around analyzing him in like microscopic detail, and he gets to be the one with other things on his mind.

Rickie: That is deep.

I feel like I could sit here on stupid fucking Park Avenue talking to him all night. And I *hate* Midtown, and I particularly hate the East Side.

Alas, wherever I'm going to figure this Nick guy out, it won't be at this spot any longer. We're two straight-edge B&T kids chasing a natural high, but apparently we've been mistaken for terrorists. Building security men have come outside to give us our marching orders—to anywhere that's not sitting at the fountain in front of their building.

We stand up and walk, heading west. Maybe Nick is trying to figure out the pieces of me, too? He says, "Your dad, the record company executive who's all about downtown. Is there a reason you haven't told me his name? Would I know who he is?"

"You would," I tell him. I need to determine which way Nick swings before I find out if he's getting to know me just so he can pass on a demo. I can only let myself get so emotionally invested.

He lets the name issue drop, mercifully. "You must meet a lot of famous people."

"Maybe when I was younger," I say. "We went to music festivals and concerts all the time. I've lived in the same house in Englewood Cliffs my whole life, but I feel like I also partially grew up in Nashville, Memphis, New Orleans, Chicago, Seattle—anywhere that had a hot music scene, you know? I'm lucky, I have met a lot of incredible artists with Dad throughout my life, some of them legends. But something I figured out a few years ago is it's better *not* to get to know them. Because if I didn't get to know them, then I could still enjoy their music, without knowing about their exorbitant demands or careless lifestyles or how much I loved their breakout song until I found out their lead singer was making my dad's life miserable and was the reason my dad missed my spelling bee or whatever."

"That's why I like Where's Fluffy so much. They're not like that, not about the whole star trip."

"Maybe not, and I hope I don't disillusion you, champ, but Lars L. is a total junkie, Owen O. is a raging alcoholic, and Evan E.'s just plain crazy. I know—my dad tried to sign them up. But Fluffy write great songs, make great music. That's what's important, right?"

Nick shoves against my side playfully. "You're not disillusioning me. You can't look at the band members and not know that. I mean, have you listened to the lyrics of 'High Is Better Than Low'? Cuz it's not about Evan E.'s love of stiletto Manolos."

Damn, Nick knows designer shoe names. Bad sign.

Nick adds, "But that's what I love about punk music. It has a sense of humor about itself, doesn't pretend to be something it's not. It's kickass funk with a heavy-metal edge, but with a conscience."

Good recovery.

"Wanna know my secret desire?" I tease.

Nick turns to me and lifts an eyebrow, like an old-time

movie star. I'm pretty sure he doesn't tweeze or wax, but he does have suspiciously beautiful eyebrows. Or maybe I'm just smit. "Of course I want to know," he says.

"I have no songwriting talent whatsoever, but I would like to be a person who thinks up song titles, especially country music ones."

"What's your best one?"

" 'You Stole My Heart and Left It for Roadkill,' " I tell him. "Go ahead, feel free to come up with some lyrics."

My favorite song title by someone who legitimately thinks up song titles would have to be "Something About What Happens When We Talk," by Lucinda Williams, the song Mom and Dad are still slow-dancing to on their anniversaries (first date, first kiss, first let's not even talk about that, engagement, wedding, etc.—yep, they celebrate 'em all), even though they're way too old and should know better. I'm thinking about that song now, because it's so easy talking with Nick. I have to suppress every stalker instinct in me not to sing to Nick like Lucinda sings, *Conversation with you is like a drug*. With Tal, discussion was always two parts confrontation and one part actual talking. I loved that Tal could at least say *goodnight,* and that he cared about something other than partying, but something about what happened when Tal and I talked was more like he manifesto'd and I listened.

As we approach Seventh Avenue, we both automatically turn south, and I realize Nick and I never discussed where we were going after Park Avenue. It's like when Nick and I held hands tight at the club earlier as I led him through the crowd to the closet. Somehow we stay together. Times Square beckons us now in all its glory. Somehow our world is alive with possibility.

My cell phone is ringing again and it says *Daddy-O* and I have to take it, that's the rule for out-all-night adventures. "Do you mind?" I ask Nick. I feel bad enough I didn't answer Caroline's call when Nick asked me not to.

"Go ahead," he says, like he understands now that no call will dissuade me from this night with him. I stand under a building awning as Nick steps away to the curb to give me privacy, which I really don't need, but I appreciate the gesture anyway, though I'm unsure where his good manners land him on the sexuality meter.

"Hi, Daddy," I say into the phone.

Here I am at the crossroads of the world, with shining red-and-white neon lights and yellow taxis, humming with action and pulsing with music and people, danger and excitement, but hearing Dad's voice, it's like I am five years old again and he's tucking his little princess into bed. "You okay, sweetheart? I've got a motley crew assembled here of two band guys and an inebriated Caroline, but no Norah."

"I'm okay, Dad. Maybe I'm even great?"

"Are you going to tell me his name?"

"No."

"Are you going to be home soon?"

"No."

"Are you ever going to obey a command of mine again?"

"No."

He sighs. "Please be careful." I decide he'd probably rather not know I am standing in Times Square in the early hours of the morning with a boy I've only known for a few hours. "Mom and I will take care of Caroline. Mom's making Thom and Scot scrambled eggs right now. Nice kids."

"Dad?"

"Yeah?"

"I think I made a mistake turning down Brown."

"No shit."

"I don't know what I'm going to do now. The Tal thing, you and Mom and Caroline were right, I can't do that ever again. But now I don't know what to do."

"I'll tell you what you can do. Go to Brown next year. Your old man took the card you posted turning down the admissions offer out of our mailbox after you left the house this morning. He replaced it with an acceptance and a deposit check."

I should be grateful but I am indignant. "YOU HAD NO RIGHT! THAT IS LIKE A PERSONAL INVASION OF PRIVACY! AND IT'S A FEDERAL OFFENSE TO TAMPER WITH THE MAIL!"

Dad chuckles. "Too fucking bad. Don't be home too late." And he hangs up on me.

Maybe my dad is a fuckin' corporate hippie, but I really love that old bastard.

I can't think about what Dad did because the skies have suddenly opened up and it's a hellacious downpour, but what is Nick doing? He's dancing a jig at the curb, his arms outstretched, his face tilted upward to receive the splash. Joyful.

I don't tell Nick my call is finished. I just watch him. A

while ago when I looked at Nick, I felt inspired by the line from that Smiths song playing earlier at Camera Obscura where Morrissey sings about how *what she asked of me / at the end of the day / Caligula would have blushed*. I don't know that I care anymore about piecing together whether Nick's straight or gay or somewhere in between. I'm thinking I would like to dance in the rain with this person. I would like to lie next to him in the dark and watch him breathe and watch him sleep and wonder what he's dreaming about and not get an inferiority complex if the dreams aren't about me.

I don't know if Nick and I are going to be friends or lovers or if he's going to be Will and I'm going to be Grace, which will be disappointing along with boring, but whatever Nick and I are going to be to each other, it can't be—it won't be—just a one-night-stand thing.

I know this.

17. NICK

Singing in the rain. I'm singing in the rain. And it's such a fucking glorious feeling. An unexpected downpour and I am just giving myself into it. Because what the fuck else can you do? Run for cover? Shriek or curse? No—when the rain falls you just let it fall and you grin like a madman and you dance with it, because if you can make yourself happy in the rain then you're doing pretty alright in life. As the first drops fall, she's still on the phone and I'm watching her talk and she's just the most amazingly complicated thing, trying on all these different expressions at once—yelling angry when she's clearly happy, then pretending to be listening when she's really watching me and the rain. Then she puts the phone back in Salvatore's pocket and walks over to me. I don't know why we say the sky is opening up when it rains—like the sky has been holding back all this time, and then this is its release. And I look at her and she looks at me and it's like everything just opens up. I am feeling the raindrops drench my clothes. I am feeling the hair fall down in my eyes. But I'm also feeling this lightness and she is so fucking beautiful the way her mouth is uncertain about whether or not to smile. We are on the edge of Times Square with its beacon of lights and we are swaying as the sky is opening, and I reach out for her to be my dance partner and she accepts. So that leaves us on the sidewalk, my arm around her body. She presses close—is just staring at me—and even though I don't know what the question is, I know the answer. So I say "This," and I lean in and I kiss her right there on the edge of Times Square, the way people kiss good-bye on the street, only this is more like a hello. This.

I open my mouth and she opens my mouth and it's like she's breathing right through me. And her body is wet and it's right against mine and I want, I want, I want. She pulls back to look at me and her eyes are laughing and her eyes are serious and I know exactly how she feels. It's another question and I offer another answer, and this time her hand curves around the back of my neck and this time her body presses tighter and mine presses even tighter back. The people around us—not many, and certainly not many sober—are looking at us, and I can't help but look around a little, and I get an idea. I tell her I have an idea and I take her hand in mine and we do that thing where you weave your fingers together, here is the church here is the steeple, and I lead her into Times Square and under the lights and past the marquees until we get to the Marquis. Suddenly she's giving me this *What the fuck?* look, because what girl wants to end up at a tourist Marriott in Times Square? But I say "Trust me" and kiss her again and there are two other people in the glass elevator with us, but they get off at the eighth-floor lobby. I ask Norah what her lucky number is and she tells me, so we go to that floor. There is nobody in the halls and best of all there's no hallway music playing, and I don't see what I'm looking for and then I find it, but Norah can't wait and she's putting her hand under my collar and feeling the skin from my shoulder to my neck and that is so damn hot that I forget where we're going for a second and I just make out with her right there in the hallway, out of sight of the atrium and the glass elevators, but still careful not to lean against any doors because that might wake up the tourists inside. Instead we press against the wall and she runs her hand down my chest then at my belt she goes right back up, only under the shirt, and her fingers feel so good there. And my fingers feel her shirt and her breasts and we are both so damn soaked and so damn ready. We kiss for about five minutes more and she's a damn good kisser. She kisses my upper lip and then kisses my lower lip and I echo her—kiss her upper lip, kiss her lower lip. Then she tries to do something with her tongue that doesn't quite work but it doesn't really matter because our hands are everywhere at once and I am so into it, and after she gives up on the tongue thing I can tell she's relaxing a little more. She's losing herself, and I love all the more that she's not trying, she's just doing.

So I steer her a little down the hall until we're in front of the room that says ICE. And she laughs and I say, "C'mon," because where else do we have to go? And the room isn't that cold, there's just the noise of the soda machine to contend with. She says, "You can't be serious," and I agree that I can't be. I'm not. I say, "I'm just really into you," and then I kiss her and she finds the light switch and turns it off, and then we're just lit in Pepsi-can colors and it's like we've finally found this other kind of conversation, this conversation in gestures and pulls and pushes and breaths and grasps and teases and glimmers and rubs and expectation. "Are you okay?" I ask, and she says, "Are you?" And I say, "Yes, I am." I am more than okay. This is a great conversation.

God, I like her so much.

"Let's get you out of some of those wet clothes," she says, and she pulls at my shirt and stumbles over some of the buttons and I don't know what comes over me, but I start tickling her and that really pisses her off, but she's laughing and then gasps back the laugh, I guess so the guests won't hear. She finishes the buttons and she takes off the shirt. I take my jacket off her shoulders and she does the strangest thing—she pulls back for a second and folds it neatly, puts it almost reverently on the floor. Then I peel off the wet flannel, peel off the T-shirt underneath. She runs her fingers through the patch of hair on my chest, then follows the trail down to my belt. I have never, ever felt such desire. She takes off the belt, lets it drop to the floor. Then she unbuttons the top button of my jeans—only the top button. And I reach over to her jeans and unbutton the top button—only the top button. And I ask it again—"Are you okay?" And this time she says yes. She says she's more than okay.

We kiss like it's a form of clasping. It's not like it was in the club, when it was like she was proving something. We have nothing to prove now, nothing except that we're not afraid. That we're not going to think too much, or stop too much, or go too much. Her hand traces down the zipper line and I say, "Slow." Because this is not a rush. This is not something insignificant. This is real. This is happening. And this is ours.

I am nervous as fuck, vulnerable as anything. I can feel my chest shaking. She embraces me so her arms are behind my back, then lets her hands wander down, across that line, under my jeans, under my boxers. I wrap my arms around her, raise my hands to her back. To her neck. To her hair. Then one hand glides back, runs over her breasts, then between them, trailing down and back around. We entangle. The ice machine hums, then comes to life, the cracking crash that makes us laugh, takes us out of the moment for a moment, makes us look at each other in a naked light. That stop. That pause.

"What are we doing?" she says.

"I don't know?" I reply.

She leans into me again, her wet pants squarely on mine, and says, "Good answer."

I want to kiss her without counting the seconds. I want to hold her so long that I get to know her skin. I want, I want, I want.

Her hands slide to my hips. Her thumbs hook around my waistband.

Lowering.

Lowering.

I gasp.

18. NORAH

When did my life get so good? Was it when I agreed with a kiss to be Nick's five-minute girlfriend, or when I realized frigid was a choice rather than a truth?

This ice room is so very cold.

Nick is so very hot.

His heat—my heat—*our* heat—almost makes me forget I am still wet from the downpour, seeking refuge in the darkened ice room of a fucking Marriott with the Pepsi sign lit up, and I am without a doubt really into Nick because I am a Coke drinker, I mean I can take the Pepsi Challenge and fucking smell the difference without bothering to distinguish the two tastes in my mouth. Mmmmmm, tastes. His lips taste so good, his moist skin tastes so good, everything about him is just delicious. Now that his wet shirt is off and my face presses right here as my hands stray down there, I realize he does not smell like aromatherapy or cologne, it was probably the air freshener Toni sprayed over everyone at the bathroom back at the club. This Nick, the bare-chested one, the heavy breathing one, the kind one, the sexy as hell one, he smells musky and lovely, bathed in night rain. I can't get enough of him.

I get it—he's straight. I believe. Hallelujah! And! Amen! J.C., I owe you one!

I feel like I could drown in this, in him. He's lit by the machine he's leaning against, but I have fallen into darkness, not the darkness of the deranged or the depressed, but the darkness of the consumed, where all I see, hear, taste, feel, is the probe of our mouths and hands, the warmth of our bodies pressed against each other, the urgency of his wanting, my wanting. It's like nothing else exists in the world right now except him, me, touching, exploring, longing, needing, sharing, having. So much for my straight-edge vow, because I am drunk on our *ing*'s. If Nick's part of 'em, I want 'em, they're mine.

He pulls me back up so our lips meet again, and I'm lost all over again, lost inside his mouth, feeling his breath, feeling his heartbeat against my hand pressed on his chest. My hands want to wander all over him, but his lips are sliding so sweetly around my own, my hands can't focus. His hands focus just fine. He's definitely a breast instead of thigh man. Only his hands go slow, caressing and teasing instead of Tal-pillaging (good job on the breast tutorial, Tris), and I can feel my chest straining to high attention, wanting, more more more. Then Nick's hands move away and I want to murmur, *No no no, come back, hands,* but my mouth is too busy occupying his. As Nick's hands fumble and smooth over my back, clearly looking for a bra strap to unclasp, my lips can't bear to pull away from touching him to tell him, *Honey, it's a front-clasp bra*.

My lips go on a downward slope, from kissing his mouth,

to his chin, his neck, moving south to his chest. His hands give up on the clasp issue and move on to fingering through my hair, and I wonder how he knows that having my scalp lightly massaged like he's doing now is just this unbelievable turn-on to me.

I want him so much and I know this should wait but curiosity to test-drive my non-frigidity is going to prevail here, it's like I can't help it. My mouth pulls back from his body as I step up on tippy toes to place my mouth against his ear to whisper into it what I want to do to him, and strangely I use the polite words instead of the nasty ones, and he whispers, "Really?" like maybe he's also not so convinced we should go that far, but his quickened breath tells me he's curious for some test-driving, too. And I whisper back, "Really," because this time he did not answer, "Slow."

My brain officially leaves the ice room, as if to say, *I can't watch. You know better.*

I've got him in my hands—wow, who knew I was ambidextrous?—and my hands are feeling, feeling, feeling, and I can hear his breathing, and it's heavy and soft at the same time, like its own feral whisper. His hands trace soft lines across my wet head, encouraging the motion of my hands, and I want him as much as I want it because he and it are the same and I am so greedy, I want everything from him.

"Norah." It's so cold in here but hearing him gasp my name, I feel like I am on fire. All those Jackie Collins novels Caroline and I read in seventh grade are totally starting to make sense.

My tongue blazes his trail, moving down toward the

motion of my hands but not quite there yet; my accelerated heart rate slows down the pace of my hands. I want this, so much, but I am terrified even as I am willingly lost in it. I'm fine with doing this—no, I'm GREAT with doing this—but scared that I will do it wrong. "Norah," Nick whispers again, and I hope that maybe with him, there is no wrong way. I hope that he will trust me. My heart is pounding pounding pounding and my mouth wants to go there but my head turns upward first, wanting to make eye contact with Nick, but in the fluorescent light I see his eyes are closed, so I speak instead, and I say, "Tell me. Guide me." Because I want it to be both our instincts making this happen. And his eyes open for a moment and catch mine and through the machine glow, I see gratitude in his, and in my hands his response is even more affirmative, and okay, here I go.

Why, hello, Julio!

But some motherfucker has turned on the lights in this room and it's not even like I want to die of embarrassment. I want to die from wanting this to happen and who the hell could be so inconsiderate as to ruin my fucking moment?

An old couple stands at the entrance to the ice room. She is dressed in a quilted robe and cheap slippers and looks just like my great-aunt Hildy in Boca who hates me because she says I have a potty mouth and because one time I made the big fucking mistake of admitting that the brisket my grandma makes is better than Aunt Hildy's. He is dressed in boxer shorts and a T-shirt and, holy fucking shit, he is wearing those sock suspenders around his calves that I'm pretty goddamn sure are museum fashion artifacts. His face is crumpled and ancient, like he could be E.T.'s great-uncle, and he's carrying an ice bucket. What the fuck do these geezers need ice for at this hour?

Their gray heads need a moment to process the blue sight.

"Oh," Great-Aunt Hildy clone finally says.

"Oh, my," her husband says.

I am imagining how Nick and Norah must look to Aunt Hildy and Uncle E.T. right now, in the Polaroid snapshot of their hopefully near-senile dementia minds. Nick: shirtless, pants still on but zippers and boxers down, his hands pressed against the back of the Pepsi machine. Norah: moist hair disheveled from Nick's earlier scalp massage, wearing wet pants with the top button unfastened, and also shirtless except for the black lace bra on her bosom, just settled into kneeling position. B-U-S-T-E-D.

I hope Aunt Hildy notices how carefully I folded Salvatore's jacket. That's got to count for something.

The silence of the shock feels like an eternity until Nick glances over at Aunt Hildy and says, "Would you be a dear and shut the light off again on your way back out?"

It's her turn to say "Oh, my" now, but bless her heart, she does flick the light switch back off, but not before shooting me one parting look, and I swear in that last lingering second, I see that she recognizes my hunger because she's felt it at some point in her life, too, and she winks at me before they're gone and I feel confident that Auntie and Uncle have truly gotten some bang for their buck on their New York City vacation. Nick and I could become goodwill ambassadors for the city now that the porno shops on 42nd Street are gone. Must make mental note to contact mayor.

Darkness has been returned to us, but the moment, the heat, is over. Because Nick speaks in a normal voice instead of a whisper, and he says, "Maybe we're not ready for this yet?" His sentiment is serious—and right—yet somehow we're laughing, too, laughing at the absurdity of the situation, and maybe laughing with relief that the absurdity allowed the situation not to go further than it did.

Aunt Hildy must have sent my brain back into the room when she left it because I am reaching for my shirt and for Salvatore as Nick puts his shirt back on. I can't believe how grateful I am to have been caught. I want him so very much, but it's too soon. I have to figure, with this many stops and starts, surely this train will pull out of the station eventually. What's the big fucking rush?

We're dressed again except our clothes are still damp and we're still laughing except we're also kinda making out against the ice machine and he bumps me in just the wrong way and now ice is pouring from the machine onto the floor, all over us, it's like a fucking avalanche, and all we can do is laugh harder and run away.

We're kissing in the hallway again, against the wall.

We're kissing in the glass elevator again. We ride it up and down, up and down, still kissing. Outside the elevator, time is going on, but inside, it's stopped for us because we've got our own schedule: kissing, giggling, probing, breathing, taking, wanting, hoping. Liking.

I don't know this Norah, this risk-taker, this thrill-seeker.

I am a nice Jewish girl from Englewood Cliffs, New Jersey. I may have a potty mouth, but I do not get caught in illicit sexual encounters in Marriotts, for fuck's sake. I guess I could be open to a Ritz-Carlton or a Four Seasons, but a Marriott, no fucking way! Yet here I am. And there's nowhere else I'd rather be. What spell has this boy cast on me?

I don't know this Norah, but I like her. I'm hoping she'll hang out awhile, consider permanent asylum.

The elevator door opens on the ground floor and we're greeted and escorted out by hotel security and I suppress the urge to sit them down for a good honest discussion about our country's founding principles of civil liberties because that would take away from my time with Nick.

So Nick and I head outside, and we're holding hands, and still giggling, and still wet from the earlier rain and the sweat of our earlier encounter(s)(s)(s). And we are giddy, because dawn is here, we're at the center of the world and we're the center of our own universe, and spring is here, and the air smells wet and clean. God bless Manhattan, you know, because it must be six in the morning on a Sunday yet trash collection trucks are teeming down the street and Times Square workers in their bright-orange uniforms are cleaning up the night's excesses and not even the smell of fresh spring rain can completely wash away Eau de Times Square Urine/Trash/Vomit, but somehow this here, this now, it feels perfect.

"Where to?" Nick asks, and I say, "Home."

We've got to find Jessie the Yugo and find our way off this island.

I have so much to do. Caroline to intervene. College to plan. Nick to know. Sexual techniques to Google.

Playlists to be created. I'm already planning the one I will make for Nick after I get some sleep. I will call it "(T)rainy/Dreamy" and it will be all dreamy songs with either the words *rain* or *train* in the title because he is so beautiful in the rain and one day I would like to make love to him on a train, just not the Chicago El like that scene in that '80s movie *Risky Business* because that was way hot but seemed so unhygienic; no, we'll take a cross-country train trip with our own cabin berth with proper sheets like in an old black-and-white movie and Nick and I will call each other "darling" and read books aloud to each other at night while the train rolls through the Plains. Off the top of my head, I'm thinking my "(T)rainy/Dreamy" playlist for Nick will include "I Wish It Would Rain" by The Temptations, "Train in Vain (Stand by Me)" by The Clash, "It's Raining" by Irma Thomas, "Blue Train" by Johnny Cash followed by "Runaway Train" by Rosanne Cash (oh! I'm so clever!), "Come Rain or Come Shine" either by Dinah Washington or the Ray Charles cover (tough call—I'll decide later), and I will cap the mix off with "Friendship Train" by Gladys Knight & The Pips because that's what it's all about in the end, right?

We're walking down Seventh Avenue and I don't know if we're going to the subway or walking all the way back to the Lower East Side or what and I don't care.

"Nick?" I say.

He lifts my hand he's holding to his mouth for a quick kiss. Then, "Yeah?" he says.

I tell him, "What just happened there? I have something to tell you."

He stops walking and he doesn't drop my hand but his grip loosens a little and I can see in his eyes that he's thinking, *Now she's going to tell me she has herpes,* or worse, *She's going to deny any of this happened at all.* I can almost see the beads of worry on his forehead. "What?" he whispers.

I look him back square in the eye. I take a deep breath, solemn, and just let it out. "I'm pregnant. I don't know if it's yours or E.T.'s."

This time I don't try to hold back my smile. It's gonna come out whether I like it or not. I choose to like it.

He doesn't hold his back either. He pulls me to him, tight. He's laughing, but part of me wants to tell him to stop because that part of me is leaning against his chest and thinking, *Shit, this is not funny, because I could seriously fall in love with you.*

19. NICK

When is a night over? Is it the start of sunrise or the end of it? Is it when you finally go to sleep or simply when you realize that you have to? When the club closes or when everyone leaves? Normally, I keep these kinds of questions to myself. But this time, I ask Norah.

"It's over when you decide it's over," she says. "When you call it a night. The rest is just a matter of where the sun is in the sky. That has nothing to do with us."

We keep walking down Seventh Avenue, through the large swath of city that is still sleeping through the dawning of the day. Night-shift cabdrivers slow when they see us, then speed up again when they notice the way we're holding hands, the way we don't seem to be in any rush to be anywhere but here.

I am exhausted. It's even too exhausting to keep denying that I'm exhausted, so I let the weight fall on my bones and my thoughts. I am so fucking tired, and most of my energy is being spent on wishing that I wasn't.

"I love this light," Norah says. The city tinted as pink in waking as it is in orange and blue when it falls to sleep.

We're both a mess. Our hair drying out in every which way. My six-in-the-morning shadow. Our disheveled clothes, still looking post-lust no matter how hard we try to shevel them. (Okay, we don't try all that hard. We're proud of them.)

"Norah," I say, "I have something to ask you."

"Sure," she says.

"It's really personal. Is that okay? I mean, you don't have to tell me if you don't want to."

"Don't worry. If I don't want to, I won't."

"Okay." I pause for a second, and I can tell she thinks I'm serious, which amuses me to no end. "Here goes. Norah?" I pause again.

"Yes, Nick?"

"Can I . . . um . . ."

She's getting annoyed. "What, Nick?"

"Could you possibly . . . maybe . . . tell me your last name?"

Without a beat, she says, "Hilton."

"No, really."

"Hyatt?"

"Norah . . ."

"Marriott? Or how about Olsen? I'm the triplet they *never fucking acknowledge*."

"I see a resemblance."

"Fuck you. It's Silverberg."

"Cool."

" 'Cool,' as in you know who my father is now?"

The thought hadn't even occurred to me.

"To be honest," I say, "even with the last name, I don't know who he is. I guess I don't follow that kind of stuff. Is that okay?"

"You have no idea how okay that is," Norah answers. "Now . . . I've shown you mine, so you show me yours."

"O'Leary."

"You're Irish?"

"Not really, like in a majority way. My grandfather just happened to win the last-name lottery. I'm really Irish-British-French-Belgian-Italian-Slav-Russian-Danish. Basically, the Euro should have my face on it."

"So you're a Euro mutt?"

"With the possible exception of Luxembourg."

"Good to know."

We angle over to Sixth, then to Broadway.

"And can I get your phone number?" I ask.

Norah pulls her hand out of mine to reach into Salvatore and take out my phone.

"Here," she says, handing it over. "It's already programmed in."

I know it's totally uncool to do it, but I ask, "Do you want mine?"

"Call me," she says. And then when I don't do anything, she adds, "Right now."

So I open up my phone and check out the directory. I see Norah's added some commentary of her own—Tris's number is now labeled *That Bitch*. Norah's, however, isn't under *Norah*. But when I see Salvatore's name, I know who I'm calling.

I dial. Her ring tone springs to life.

"Hello?" she answers, not two feet away from me.

"Can I please speak to Salvatore?" I ask.

"I'm afraid he can't come to the phone right now. Would you like to leave a message?"

I'm looking at Salvatore now, and I'm realizing that I gave him up a long time ago, that in my mind he's already hers.

"Tell him I hope he likes his new home," I say.

Norah looks at me. "Are you sure?"

"Yeah, I'm sure."

"Thanks."

We both hang up and hold hands again. We walk through Union Square, stepping over the detritus of the Saturday-night revelers. We pass the Virgin Megastore, the Strand, the old Trinity Church. We walk down Astor, past the skate-punks' cube, over to St. Marks Place, where clubgoers stumble through daylight. Down Second Avenue until we reach Houston. I can tell she's tired now, too. We are using all of our energy for this walking, for this near-silent twoliness. For the watching of everything. For watching over each other.

When we get to Ludlow, I remember the song I began to write, in an hour that seems like weeks ago now. Can so much really happen in a night? The song was never really over, but now I have the ending—I don't know how I'll phrase it, but it will involve our returning, it will take in the strange pink light and the Sunday-morning quiet. Because the song is us, and the song is her, and this time I'm going to use her name. Norah Norah Norah—no rhymes, really. Just truth.

I shouldn't want the song to end. I always think of each night as a song. Or each moment as a song. But now I'm seeing we don't live in a single song. We move from song to song, from lyric to lyric, from chord to chord. There is no ending here. It's an infinite playlist.

I know Norah would love for me to sing her the song, right here on Ludlow Street. But I'll wait for next time. Because I know there will be a next time. I was looking forward to next time the minute I met her. Throughout the night, I've been looking forward to next time, and the time after that, and the time after that. I know this is something.

I can see Jessie sitting safely at the curb, ready to take us home.

"We're almost there," Norah says.

I stop us. We turn to each other and kiss again. Here on Ludlow Street. In the new day.

My heartbeat accelerates. I am in the here, in the now. I am also in the future. I am holding her and wanting and knowing and hoping all at once. We are the ones who take this thing called music and line it up with this thing called time. We are the ticking, we are the pulsing, we are underneath every part of this moment. And by making the moment our own, we are rendering it timeless. There is no audience. There are no instruments. There are only bodies and thoughts and murmurs and looks. It's the concert rush to end all concert rushes, because this is what matters. When the heart races, this is what it's racing toward.

20. NORAH

I can keep the jacket, I can keep the jacket, lalalalalalalala, Nick loves me, or at least he really likes me, lalalalalalalala, Salvatore and I are so happy, this jacket will only be dry cleaned, no inferior detergent shall ever besmirch it, lalalalalalalala.

Here we are, back in Jessie. Yugo! Lalalalalalalala.

I'm sitting in the passenger seat next to Nick and it's just like before when we sat side by side in this car, except not. I'm no longer vague as to whether I even want to be spending my time with this person, in this "vehicle," but Jessie, like earlier, has doubts about whether to allow me to be Jessie's Girl. Jessie, once again, is not starting. Nick turns the key and floods the accelerator and even says a couple prayers, but no, Jessie ain't putting out.

Nick stops the key motion and turns to look at me. "Shit," he says.

I can't help but laugh at the sight of him, rumpled clothes, his hair spiked from the rain and the mad earlier rummage of my hands through it, eyes glazed over from the fallout of lust and fatigue, jaw jutted in frustration with Jessie. I tell him, "You look like that Where's Fluffy song, 'You Have That Just Fucked Look, Yoko,'" which I believe was on the breakup desolation playlist Nick made for Tris, and in my opinion is the band's best song from their pre–Evan E. days, when Fluffy's drummer was a guy called Gus G., who left them in a fit of rage when Lars L. dumped the band's manager, who also happened to be Gus G.'s girlfriend.

"Oh, be still my heart, Norah," Nick says. Then, seriously, he says, "Dev claims 'I Wanna Hold Your Hand' is the ultimate song because it captures the essence of what every pop song is really about, what we all really want—simply, I Wanna Hold Your Hand." Nick takes his right hand from the stick shift and clasps my left hand. "I think Dev might be on to something."

"I hate The Beatles," I state. "Except for that song 'Something.' Now that's a fucking love song. And John or Paul didn't even write it. George did. George was the shit. But The Beatles as a whole? Completely overrated."

Nick drops my hand. He looks at me as if either I've just had a mental breakdown, or he's about to have one. "I'm gonna pretend I never heard that."

Musician boys and their Beatles love—what are ya gonna do? I lean over to place a make-up kiss on his neck. Then I ask, "Did you really write a song for me?"

"Yeah. But it's not finished. And don't ever speak of The Beatles with such condescension again or I may never finish it."

"So do I get to hear it, even the unfinished version?"

"No."

"Never? Or just not now?"

"Just not now. Don't be so greedy." He knows me so well already.

He turns the key again. And again and again and again. "Shit," he repeats.

"What are our options?" I ask.

"Well, we can try to find someone to jump the car. Or we can just leave her here and find our way home on the train and worry about Jessie after some sleep. I could come back later today with Thom and Scot to jump her. Or, you know . . . I could always admit that Jessie has broken my heart for the last time, and give her away to charity already."

Poor Nick. Tris broke his heart. Jessie broke his heart.

I whisper in his ear, "I promise I will never break your heart." Because without a doubt, I will fuck up many things in this whatever-we-have-here, but that, I will never do.

"Uh, thank you?" Nick whispers back.

I'm probably wading close to stalker territory again, so I decide to shut up. Then he leans over and places his hand around the back of my neck and pulls me to him to kiss me again. It's amazing how often captives start to associate with their captors. And I try the tongue thing again, the yin, the yang, the sucking and pulling, and this time he finds my frenulum all on his own, and check us out, we're starting to find our rhythm with this. My chakras feel very, very open and Jessie's windows are looking very, very steamed.

But I pull away because if we don't stop this already, we'll never get home. "Tell you what, Nick," I say. "You keep trying to coax a start out of Jessie, and I'll go into the Korean grocery and see if anyone in there can help us."

I step outside the car and some bum is singing "Ride Like the Wind" against a wall and I give him my very last buck to stop. I go inside the store, where I'm supposed to be finding someone to help us with jumper cables, but I'm really standing around debating whether to just call Dad—or better yet, Dad's assistant—and ask for a call to be placed to a car service to come get us; that method has gotten Caroline and me home on many occasions. With one phone call, I could make this so easy for me and Nick. And if I'm not placing that call as I stand here with my teeth chattering in the freezer section, I'm not sure if it's because I don't want Nick to think I'm a princess or because I am trying to buy more time with him.

Nick asked for my phone number, but he never said *when* he was going to call me. We've only known each other a few hours, yet we've, um, gotten to know each other pretty well I'd say, so I would hope it would at least be implied that we're going to see each other again soon, but he never said *when*. And I don't like waiting to find out.

I pull my phone from Salvatore's pocket and review the call log. I see Nick's number. I debate whether to assign a name to his number. If I commit to that, then I will truly be heartbroken if he never calls me again; my heart will knot each and every time I use this phone and see his name in there. I would probably end up having to trash the phone entirely. Then I hear the song on the radio at the counter and it's Dad's beloved ol' Alanis and I think how in one night Nick inspired what Dad calls my "Norah-as-Alanis teenage transformations," in which Dad says I am capable of instantly converting from raging wildcat "You Oughta Know" Alanis into tender pussycat "Thank U" Alanis, and I decide to program Nick into my phone anyway, despite my misgivings. I consider assigning his number the name *NoMo,* but suspect that would really piss him off. *Salvatore's babydaddy* would take too long to get in there. So I just key in *Nick*. So simple. So sweet. And I call him.

"Did you find anyone in there with jumper cables?" he asks, hopeful.

"Didn't ask anyone yet. So, like, if you're going to call me, can you let me know when that would be?"

"You're not leaving me room for the element of surprise."

"I hate surprises."

"I don't believe you."

"Listen," I say, serious. "Did Tris ever do that thing with you where she called you from the backseat of your car while you were driving her? Cuz she learned that one from me. That bitch isn't always the teacher, you know."

"Tris who?" he says, and hangs up on me. I am glad I programmed his name for keeps.

I hope Nick has money on him because I am truly using the very last of my dough now, paying in quarters and dimes and pennies for another bag of stale Oreos, and as I shove the coins to the counter person, I shout, for all in the store to hear, "DOES ANYONE FUCKING HAVE A CAR WITH JUMPER CABLES IN HERE OR WHAT?"

No response. Hey, I gave it my best shot. Before I return to the car, though, I listen to the voice mail Caroline left earlier in the night. She must have called during her post-heave stage just before she went to bed, because her voice is all cuddly and happy. "Norah? Norah Norah Norah," she sings in a whisper, like a lullaby. "Thom and Scot said you're on a date with their friend! That Nick guy was cute, even if he did wear ugly shoes. And you must really like him if you're not answering this call, because I know you, and I know you know I am calling you. And I guess all I want to say to you is, you're always taking care of me and even though it was kinda weird to wake up in a dark van with two strange guys in the parking lot of some fucking 7-Eleven, I'm also glad you're taking care of yourself instead of me for once. And I hope you're having a great time, I really do. And tomorrow afternoon when I am hung over and cursing you out for abandoning me, you just play me back this message, okay, bitch? Love you." I smile. And save the message.

I go back to Jessie. "Sorry, fella," I tell Nick when I get back into the car. I offer him a stale Oreo.

"I hate Oreos," he says, and now it's my turn to say, "I'm gonna pretend I never heard that."

Nick steps out of Jessie to open the hood. While he's inspecting the engine, I inspect the notebook of CDs laying on the floor. There's the usual suspects in there, Green Day and The Clash and The Smiths, yeah, but there's also Ella and Frank, even Dino, some Curtis Mayfield and Minor Threat and Dusty Springfield and Belle & Sebastian, and as I flip through his musical life, getting to know him through his tastes, I must acknowledge that not only am I not frigid, but I also may be multi-orgasmic. This Nick guy may never call me again after all, but he's my fucking musical soulmate. I take his portable boom box from the backseat and program a wake-up jam.

Nick steps back inside the car. "That's it," he says. "We've got to figure out another plan to get home. Jessie's not going anywhere." He pulls his wallet out. "And of course I have no money left. But I do have a MetroCard! I'm so sorry, Norah."

I'm not sorry, because his words have made me think of my favorite Le Tigre song. I mumble, "My! My MetroCard!" and Nick picks up the song by answering with a call of, "OH FUCK / Giuliani," and we both finish with, "HE'S SUCH / A fucking jerk!"

"Let's just leave Jessie here for today. I'll figure out what to do with her after some sleep. If we hop the A train to Port Authority, I know a guy there who drives the early morning van service to Hoboken. He's in Pretty Girls Named Jen, the hardcore screamo band from Jersey City—do you know them? Anyway, I know he'll give us a free ride, and once we get back to Hoboken I can take my sister's car and drive you home. So all we have to do is get to the A train. Though I'm not sure I have the energy to walk all the way to the A train. You?"

At this point, we've completely forfeited a night's sleep so we might as well wake the hell up and enjoy this brand-new day. I respond with a single word: "BEASTIE!" I hit play on the CD player, and like that, Nick and I are singing along together, wailing out "I like to party, not drink Bacardi" and just all-out grooving to "Triple Trouble," because we've got the Beastie funk and it's damn pleasant and getting louder and louder as we rock Jessie. Nick is head thrashing and I am head thrashing and together we are Johnny Castle meets Johnny Rotten via DJ Norah caffeine jolt. And we are awake, and alive.

We make the long walk to Canal Street—make that, we almost sprint there—and we're holding hands and laughing and kissing and sing-shouting, "Mommy's just jealous it's the BEASTIE BOYS," and like that we're there and we're skipping down the steps into the station. Some spray-painted graffiti on the wall asks, *Is it nothing to you, all you who pass by? Lamentations 1:12* and I think, *No, Lord, whoever the hell You are, this is not nothing to me. This counts.* Like, I could see myself being one of those tourists in Chinatown and I could buy a shirt that says, "I Survived the All-Nighter" or "Nick & Norah Went to the Marriott Marquis and All I Got Was This Lousy Shirt," as if the experience never happened without the T-shirt to prove it.

Nick slides the MetroCard through the turnstile and we hear a train approaching and it's early Sunday morning so I better hurry because who knows how long it will be before another train comes through. He passes the card to me but when I try to slide it through, the machine reads *Insufficient Fare,* because Nick must have just used the last value of the card.

"Fuck!" I say.

"Fuck!" he says.

Nick puts his hand on mine from the other side of the turnstile. He says, "Don't worry about it, just jump over."

I hesitate even though I know my wavering could cost us the approaching train. If I make this jump, then this is real, he is real. I will have broken the law for him and that will bind us together forever, outlaws, like Bonnie and Clyde. And look how that worked out for them.

"C'mon, Norah," Nick says. I hear his urgency, and once again, I think, *Oh, poor Nick*. I mean, I think I am basically a cool girl, but I am also a pain in the ass. I know this. It's like he has no idea what he's setting himself up for. I should just call the car service for myself and let Nick go.

"Norah?"

If I do this, it will be like jumping into the middle of the mosh pit. Dangerous. Exhilarating. Terrifying. It's only a fucking turnstile, but what if I don't make it to the other side. Some people never make it out of the mosh alive.

The deafening screech of train brakes announces the train is in the station.

Nick says, "Are we in this or not?"

To throw myself into the breach of our great divide will be a leap of faith.

I grab hold of his warm hand. Deep breath.

Ready.

Set.

Jump.

ABOUT THE AUTHORS

Rachel Cohn & David Levithan are not Nick and Norah, though Rachel wrote Norah's part and David wrote Nick's. Both are highly acclaimed young adult authors in their own right and are writing together for the first time.

Rachel's previous books include *Gingerbread,* an ALA Best Book for Young Adults, an ALA Top Ten Quick Pick for Young Adults, and a *Publishers Weekly* and *School Library Journal* Best Book of the Year, as well as its sequel, *Shrimp*.

David's previous books include *Boy Meets Boy,* an ALA Top Ten Best Book for Young Adults, an ALA Quick Pick, and a Lambda Literary Award winner; *The Realm of Possibility,* an ALA Top Ten Best Book for Young Adults; and *Are We There Yet?*

Rachel lives in New York City and David lives in Hoboken, New Jersey. If traffic is good, it only takes a half hour to bus and subway between their apartments.

Their Web sites are linked—www.rachelcohn.com and www.davidlevithan.com. Also make sure to check out www.nickandnorah.com.